# THE
# PICTURE-
# PERFECT
# MURDERS

# THE PICTURE-PERFECT MURDERS

Created by Bill Adler
Written by Thomas Chastain

*Photographs by Marjory Dressler*

WILLIAM MORROW AND COMPANY, INC.
*New York*

Library of Congress Cataloging-in-Publication Data

Chastain, Thomas.
    The picture-perfect murders.
    1. Literary recreations.  I. Adler, Bill.  II. Title.
PS3553.H3416P5  1987      813'.54       85-15480
ISBN 0-688-04797-1

Printed in the United States of America

First Edition

1 2 3 4 5 6 7 8 9 10

BOOK DESIGN BY BERNARD SCHLEIFER

# AUTHORS' NOTE

IT IS NOT OFTEN, when a series of connected murders occurs, that an extensively documented photographic and written record is assembled—step by step—of the evidence. In this book the reader will find such a record included in the text of what became known as *The Picture-Perfect Murders.*

This photographic and written record was compiled by two individuals, George Preston and Kenneth McCallum, who participated in most of the events surrounding the murders. It was their thought that perhaps one day they would publish their own version of the mystifying pieces-of-eight puzzle. To this end, George Preston kept a written record of much of what transpired, while Kenneth McCallum—who was an amateur photographer—was responsible for a collection of photographs pertaining to the deaths. Their book was never published.

However, many of the notes and photographs put together by them are included in this book and were used by the private investigator John Lange in his attempt to solve the eight murders recounted in the following pages.

—BILL ADLER
THOMAS CHASTAIN

*New York City*

# PHOTO PAGES

(AUTHORS' NOTE: *Most of the photographs in this book appear alongside the text where reference is made to them. There were, however, certain miscellaneous photographs collected by Kenneth McCallum that do not seem to fit into any specific section of the story. These photographs are included on the following pages. . . .*)

7

# Torso Murder Puzzles Police

Police admitted being baffled by the discovery of a headless female whose decaptiated body was discovered inside a trunk alongside the expressway late last night.

A passing motorist, Jack

Photo of a ragged newspaper clipping about a murder case . . .

42     ERLE STANLEY GARDNER

one of the seats in the cabin. His knee was in my stomach. His right hand was trying to choke me. I had twisted my shoulders around so I could bite at his wrist and keep him from getting a good hold on my throat. Both of my hands were clawing at his bare arm."

"Bare?" Mason asked.

"Yes."

"Did he have any clothes on?"

"Just his underwear."

"What happened?"

"Someone called something, and I think Wentworth must have looked up at the skylight, and then—then bang, it happened."

"Kill him instantly?"

"He rolled off the cushioned seat, doubled up with his hands over his face, and ran aft out of the cabin."

"Then what?" Mason asked.

"I looked up and could see someone moving. I heard steps on the deck. I ran back to the door that goes to the after cabin. I called out to Penn to ask if he was hurt. He didn't answer. I tried to open the door. He must have been lying against it. I couldn't push it open."

"It opened into the after cabin?"

"That's right."

"Then what?" Mason asked.

"Then I ran up on deck."

"Where did you meet Anders?"

"On the deck," she said, shifting her eyes quickly.

Mason scowled and glanced at Anders.

Anders said, "Here, let me tell this, Mae."

"By all means," Mason said.

"I distrusted this man, Wentworth. I thought he might

THE CASE OF THE POSTPONED MURDER     43

know where Mae was or that Mae might try to get in touch with him. I went down to the Yacht Club where he keeps his boat."

"So you found her?"

"Yes. About nine-thirty she drove up to the Yacht Club."

"What happened?" Mason asked.

"She left the car and went aboard, and I . . . well, I . . ."

"Go ahead," Mason said impatiently. "What did you do?"

"I lost my nerve," Anders admitted. "I thought she'd gone aboard voluntarily and—and that perhaps she'd thank me to keep out of her business."

"A wise assumption," Mason said. "Let's have the rest of it."

"Well, I sat there, feeling like a heel, lower than a snake's belly, and—"

"For the love of Mike," Mason interrupted. "I know how you felt. I know the thoughts that were going through your mind. I want facts! We may have to move fast. What happened? Give it to me straight from the shoulder and fast."

"I heard Mae scream," Anders said. "I jumped out of the car and started toward the yacht. She screamed again. The yacht was tied to a float. There's a walk running the length of the float, and then a lot of U-shaped stalls. . . ."

"I know all about that," Mason said. "You don't need to go into those details."

"No, but it's important," Anders insisted. "You see, Mr. Mason, my eyes were blinded by watching the lights on the yacht, and I was running fast—"

"—and he fell in," Mae Farr interposed.

"I fell in," Anders said.

Photo of part of a page of an Erle Stanley Gardner novel . . .

Photo of a torn matchbook cover stamped "Aspen, Colorado". . .

Photo of a key tag—with no key—stamped "Room 314". . .

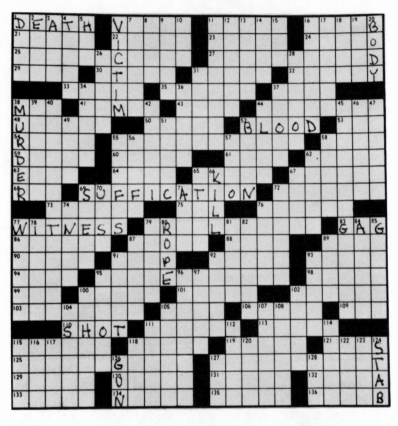

Photo of crossword puzzle with some of the words filled in . . .

Photo of a single cufflink with initial "L" . . .

Photo of woman's black wig on a wig holder . . .

# CHAPTER ONE

WHEN GEORGE PRESTON and his wife, Dina, planned their gala New Year's Eve party, it is not likely the thought ever crossed their minds that it would mark not only the start of the year but also of the series of murders that would take place around them in the coming months.

The setting for the party was the Preston estate in Southampton, Long Island, in New York.

While they were dressing for the evening, Dina asked her husband anxiously: "Are you *sure* this party isn't going to be too much for you to handle?"

George gave her a reassuring smile. "Not at all. What is there for me to do, after all, except be charming? This isn't going to be a cutthroat board of directors' meeting—yet—where they hand me my head and push me out the door."

"I suppose not," Dina murmured, the doubt still in her voice.

They were in the master bedroom. Dina, in front of the mirror, fastened a strand of pearls around her neck. George, standing behind her, looked at her reflection in the mirror and nodded his approval at her appearance.

Her gown was simple, black silk, set off by small ruffles around the hem and the wrist-length sleeves. What her appearance expressed, Dina was: neat, smart, worth a second look.

She gave George a quick kiss on the cheek and left the room, saying she was going to check on the last minute preparations being made by the butler and the maids.

George said, "I'll be right down," and took her place in front of the mirror. As he straightened the bow of his tie and slipped on his dinner jacket, he admitted to himself that Dina had good cause for some anxiety about the evening's party; the truth was, he did, too.

The problem was that almost all of the guests who would be at the party that night were connected in one way or another with the multimillion-dollar Hitchling Health Foods Company and would—if they had their way—like to replace him as president and chairman of the board of the company. Or, as some proposed, to sell the company and pocket the profits. Both moves had been opposed by George Preston. The biggest problem Preston faced was that the rest of the board of directors was made up of two different family groups who had bought into the company and onto the board. Now they were fighting him, and among themselves, for control of Hitchling, which was the world's largest health foods company.

One of the family groups was the Durbins: a widowed mother, Irene; her son, Richard; daughter, Valerie; and son-in-law, Arthur Carrolton.

For a time, Richard Durbin had headed up the company's office in London—where he had taken a wife, Joanna. He was now a member of the board working in Hitchling Health Foods' Manhattan headquarters.

Valerie, Irene's daughter, had married Arthur Carrolton, who had once run the Toronto, Canada, office and was presently working in the Manhattan headquarters. Both Valerie and Arthur were board members.

Irene Durbin, mother of Richard and Valerie, although not on the board, was always scheming to place her son or son-in-law at the head of the company.

The other family group, the McCallums, were equally eager to wrest away control of the company.

The McCallum family consisted of Judith McCallum Justin, her two sons, and a daughter: Evan McCallum and Kenneth and Karen McCallum, who were twins. Evan and Kenneth both served on the board of Hitchling Health Foods.

All of these people would be guests for the New Year's Eve party, except for Richard and Joanna Durbin.

George Preston, still in his forties, still rugged in

appearance, had no intention of giving up control of the company without a determined fight—if it came to that. George smoothed down the lapels of his jacket, turned from the mirror, and went downstairs to join his wife.

Somewhat later on that bitterly cold last day of December and of the old year, an ice storm laid a frozen glaze across the grounds of the Preston estate. In the wintry early darkness, the warm glow of lights from inside the house was reflected in the chill outside; in icicles dripped from the eaves of the horse barn and from the ice-sheathed steel mesh fences enclosing the drained swimming pool and the tennis courts stripped of their nets. Wind off the Atlantic Ocean, not far away, blew an icy spray against the windows of the house.

Fortunately, most of the guests who were expected had arrived before the onset of the storm.

John Lange, the last to appear, was shown by the butler, Edward, into the library. The others had already gathered, drinks in hand, around the great stone fireplace where a warming fire blazed.

Lange, who had been a captain in the homicide bureau of the New York City Police Department, had since retired. Presently, he worked as head of security for Hitchling Health Foods. In addition to their working relationship, John Lange and George Preston were personal friends.

As George Preston led Lange around the library to introduce, or re-introduce, him to the others assembled there, Lange—out of long habit—mentally registered his impressions of each in turn.

"You remember Judith, of course," George said.

"Of course." Lange shook hands with Judith once-McCallum (reminding himself that she had remarried since being widowed, but her new last name escaping him at the moment).

She was still a handsome woman, as he'd remembered, her face smooth-skinned and good-boned, her well-preserved looks helped in no small part by her hair colored—he had no doubt—several years younger than its roots. Her striking gown, an emerald taffeta, could no better proclaim it was the expensive work of a name designer than if its creator's label was stitched across the front of the bodice instead of inside the back of the collar. Clearly, in wearing the gown, Judith was out to outdo the dress of the other ladies present.

Lange's lapse of memory about Judith's current last name was answered by George's next introduction.

William Justin, the new husband, gave Lange a calculated bone-crushing handshake, a macho gesture so clichéd that Lange almost laughed in the man's face at the adolescence of the mind behind the muscle. Justin had graying-to-white hair, a face with the slightly jaundiced pallor of a sunlamp tan, and a stomach that had been squeezed into his stout-size tuxedo trousers. "Hi ya," Justin said, and turned away.

"I don't believe you've ever met Evan Mc-Callum," George Preston said, steering Lange to the next two guests, "and Evan's fiancée, Liza Parkland."

"Oh, yes, John Lange," Evan McCallum said, nodding, "how are you there?" The tone of his voice was as remote as if he were speaking to Lange over a telephone. A man of medium height and build, Evan McCallum was in his late thirties and had a thin face and a head of hair, sandy-colored, to match.

Liza Parkland, on the other hand, had plenty of everything: blonde hair, bosom, bottom, long legs, all nicely shaped and shown to advantage in the tight fitting mauve gown with the skirt split up one side.

"Hello," she said softly, taking Lange's hand in both of hers. "Nice to see you."

"Hello," Lange said and thought, *how nice to see so much of you.*

He wouldn't have minded lingering longer there, but George was moving him on around the room to another couple—Irene Durbin, whom he knew, standing with a man he didn't know.

As Lange and Irene exchanged greetings, he couldn't help noticing that the weight she'd put on since he'd last seen her made her appear even more the indulged dowager he'd always thought her to be. Her silver hair looked like a metallic helmet atop her head, the metallic effect carried out as well in the silver sequinned gown she wore.

George was saying something about the man with Irene, introducing him to Lange as Dr. Francke.

"They tell me you were a detective," Dr. Francke said to Lange. "Interesting."

*A burned-out case* was Lange's impression of the

doctor with sagging jowls, sallow complexion, and shiny tuxedo.

Before George could steer Lange on around the room, Edward, the butler, appeared to announce that dinner was served.

On the way into the dining room, George introduced Lange to the twins, Kenneth and Karen McCallum. Lange was startled by their striking looks and uncanny resemblance to one another. He judged them to be in their late twenties, dark-haired, hers short for a girl, his long for a boy—both worn in a kind of page boy style. So closely matched were they physically that as Lange looked from one to another *she* could have been her brother in drag and he could have been *her* in a tailored tuxedo.

In the dining room, as they took their places around the table, Lange paused to speak to Valerie Carrolton and her husband, Arthur, both of whom he knew.

These two had always amused Lange: she, black-haired with a sweet face and a shy, almost self-effacing manner; he, appearing to be slightly bored by it all. This was amusing to Lange because he knew her to be an extremely efficient and calculating person and Arthur to be concealing an inward, driving, ambitious nature.

The main course of the dinner—there were seven courses, quite properly—was goose, served with truffles and a dozen various vegetable and potato dishes and a nearly equal number of bottles of wine.

It wasn't until they were finishing their desserts that Judith suddenly cried out in a distressed voice:

"Oh, I've only just realized that there are exactly thirteen of us here—"

"Yes, we know," Dina said quickly. "We invited a fourteenth guest. I don't know what's happened to her. Perhaps she's still on the way. I didn't want to delay dinner—"

"But thirteen!" Judith said, shaking her head. "It's an unlucky way to start the new year."

"Come come, Mrs. Justin," Dr. Francke said loudly, "surely you don't believe in that superstitious nonsense?"

"Besides," Evan said, "it's still the old year. Perhaps the number will change before midnight."

After dinner they all returned to the library, this time taking places in a semicircle of chairs arranged around the fireplace. Edward served them after-dinner drinks while they waited for the approach of midnight.

They could hear from outside the shriek of the wind and the sound of sleet bouncing off the windowpanes.

"Since we have to entertain ourselves a bit," George said, looking around at the others and then fixing his eyes on Lange, "I wonder if you'd tell us what—during your years of investigating crime—was your most interesting case?"

"I—uh—" Lange shifted uneasily in his chair. Always the outsider, the observer, Lange was never comfortable when he was the center of attention. Quite ordinary looking, he would have said of himself, nothing much there to catch the eye—which was the way he wanted it to be.

As he still hesitated to speak, Dr. Francke and several of the others also began to urge him to tell about his most interesting case. Finally, he nodded.

"It is not difficult for me to remember," Lange said slowly, "since it was the first murder case I worked on after I joined the police in Massachusetts, the first police job I had."

The case, he explained, had occurred many years before on Cape Cod. The setting was in a community of summer homes, a community so small it had no name, on the Cape. Most of the people who had houses there only occupied them during the summer months, when they fished and sailed; when the summer ended, the people returned to Boston or New York or other cities where they lived.

A young woman—he'd call her Kathleen, although that was not her real name, he said—was one of these people.

She was in her thirties, a quite plain-looking woman, but also quite rich, an heiress. Her family had been in the textile business in Massachusetts, and she had inherited a fortune while she was in her late twenties, after her parents died.

About a year prior to the events he was going to describe, Lange said, Kathleen met a young man, was swept off her feet by him, and they married. He'd call the man Howard, although that was not his real name either, Lange added.

The summer of the first year of their marriage,

Kathleen and Howard came to the house she owned on the Cape. It was a comfortable place, set right at the edge of the bay with a boathouse and pier. The couple did a lot of entertaining of their summer neighbors and were quite popular in the community.

"The husband, Howard, was especially popular with the young ladies," Lange said, and cleared his throat with a slight cough.

In fact, it soon became apparent that Howard was mixed up with several of the young ladies in the area, all of whom found him handsome and engaging.

Naturally, there were quarrels between Kathleen and her husband, quarrels known to their neighbors and acquaintances and to the local woman who came in by day to clean for them. But the couple always seemed to patch up their differences.

And so the summer wore on. Until what might be called the fateful night, Lange said.

On that particular summer's night there was a violent storm. As had so frequently been the case that summer, Kathleen and Howard were again entertaining their neighbors, ten or twelve of them. There was a lot of drinking going on. In the midst of it, Kathleen and Howard had a big row right in front of their guests. Kathleen ran from the house into the storm, and Howard ran after her. The guests watched the two of them disappear down the pier into the boathouse. Somewhat sobered by this domestic spat, the guests left and went home.

Lange paused in his story, took a sip of brandy

from the glass he was holding, and then went on with the story.

By the next morning the storm had passed. When the local woman arrived to clean the house, the lights were still on in most of the rooms, but there was no sign of either Kathleen or Howard. The woman was understandably uneasy but not yet alarmed.

She went about straightening up the house and only after a time finally went down to the boathouse where, on occasion, Kathleen and Howard also entertained guests. The scene inside was in total disarray. The wicker furniture, chairs, table, chaise lounge, and the bamboo bar were overturned. There was a smashed liquor bottle on the floor and some spots of blood.

"Now thoroughly alarmed," Lange said, "the woman called the police."

The police, Lange among them, arrived promptly. They went to work immediately collecting and analyzing possible evidence from the wreckage in the boathouse. At the same time the police ascertained that a car belonging to the couple was missing from the garage. They sent out to police statewide a description of the car, while the Motor Vehicles Bureau in Boston went to work obtaining the license plate number to the car, which was owned by the wife.

"Jumping ahead in the story," Lange said, "I will tell you the blood found in the boathouse matched Kathleen's blood type and that hairs found on the jagged edges of the smashed liquor bottle were her hairs, all of which was determined somewhat later."

21

On that day, it was not until some hours later that Howard showed up at the house. When the police questioned him as to the whereabouts of his wife, he said he didn't know.

His story was that, yes, he and Kathleen had quarreled the previous night in the boathouse—although he denied striking her with a liquor bottle—and she said she was going to leave him. He had left her in the boathouse and gone back to the main house. When he found that all the others had left, he went to bed. The next morning when he got up, he discovered she was nowhere around and that the car was gone.

He claimed he'd hitchhiked a ride into Boston, where he'd spent several fruitless hours looking for her and for the car. Finally he had given up and caught the bus back to the summer house, where the police were waiting.

The police grilled Howard but couldn't shake his story. On the other hand, he couldn't prove he had hitchhiked into Boston. A day later the car was found parked on a street in midtown Boston.

Police suspected that Howard himself had driven the car into Boston and left it there so it would appear she had been the one to have done so. Then he took the bus back.

It was the police theory that Howard had killed Kathleen and dumped her body either in the bay or somewhere between the summer house and Boston.

A search was made for the body but turned up nothing.

Although the police had no corpse to prove there

had been a murder committed, they did believe they had sufficient *corpus delicti*—substantial and fundamental facts to prove the commission of the crime—to try Howard. And there *were* such precedents in law.

"So," Lange said softly, "Howard was brought to trial, found guilty by a jury, and sentenced to die in the electric chair. After several appeals, he was put to death."

Lange smiled slightly and looked around the room.

"It's a good story all right," George said.

Lange nodded. "Only that's not the end of it."

When some time had passed after Howard's execution, Lange said, Kathleen suddenly reappeared.

*Her* story was that after the night of the fight in the boathouse, she decided she had to get away for a while. Since she hadn't wanted Howard to know where she was, she drove to Boston, left the car there, and caught a plane to Mexico. She claimed that during all the time Howard was on trial and was executed, she was living in a remote area of Mexico and had no way of knowing what was going on. She expressed shock that Howard had died in the electric chair for her murder. She explained that the incriminating evidence in the boathouse, the blood and her hairs on the smashed liquor bottle, resulted when she tripped and fell, knocking the bottle to the floor and then cutting her head superficially on the broken bottle.

"That poor, poor woman. She must have felt just awful," Valerie said sadly.

23

Lange looked at Valerie owlishly. "Oh, I think not," he said. "After all, she had committed the perfect murder, don't you see?"

It was quiet in the room for a moment before George said, "Murder's such a fascinating subject."

"Except for the victim," Lange pointed out.

Dina and George had planned that at midnight they all would have champagne and caviar in the library. Edward Garrick, the butler, and his wife, Julia, who was the housekeeper, would be in the kitchen with a TV set tuned to the scene of the ball dropping in Times Square. At the stroke of midnight, Edward would flick the lights off and on in the library to signal the New Year.

Shortly before 11:30 P.M., Edward began to prepare the champagne and caviar in the library. Most of the guests and the host and hostess went to their various rooms—all of the guests were staying overnight—to freshen up before the toast was drunk.

Lange remained in the library as Edward moved soundlessly around the room with glasses, bottles, and dishes. Then the butler left the room. Lange strolled back and forth, inspecting the guns in a cabinet on one side of the room, the shelves of books on another side. Suddenly, without warning, Lange was interrupted in his perusal of the guns and books by the sound of a woman's terrified scream from somewhere on the upper floor.

He hurried from the library to the great hall outside. Looking up, he saw Dina leaning over the bannisters at the top of the circular staircase which swept upward from the hall to the second floor. Dina was still screaming and now Lange could understand her words.

"Help!" she cried. "Come quickly! Something terrible has happened to Judith! She's dead!"

Lange raced up the stairs as others came hurrying from rooms all along the corridor on the second floor. Dina was standing in front of a closed door right at the top of the stairs. She was pointing toward the door.

"What is it?" Lange asked.

"Judith!" Dina repeated, almost hysterical. "She's— been murdered! In there!"

Karen, Judith's daughter, gave a cry and started to open it.

"Wait!" Lange ordered sharply, stopping Karen.

As some of the others started toward the door, Lange spoke again: "Clear back everyone! Don't go in till I've taken a look."

He brushed past the group and opened the door, stepping into the room so his back prevented anyone else from entering until he had a chance to examine the scene.

What he saw was a bedroom that looked quite tidy and neat except that the French doors leading to a second floor terrace stood open, with a pane of glass in one of the doors shattered and pieces of glass lying on the floor. Also a woman's handbag lay on the carpet in the center of the room, the handbag's contents spilled across the carpet. What he didn't see was a body.

25

*Southampton Police photo titled: "Scene of the murder"*

26

Puzzled, Lange turned and spoke to Dina rather more sharply than he'd intended: "What's going on? There's no sign of Judith in here. Where did you see her?"

"No sign?" Dina asked, her voice sounding as puzzled as Lange's had. "But I saw her. Lying on the floor. In the room—"

"Where? Where?" Lange demanded impatiently, moving aside, now urging Dina closer. Some of the others crowded around the doorway.

Dina entered the doorway fearfully, looked into the room, and then slowly shook her head as if bewildered.

"But I saw her," Dina said. She pointed to a spot near where the handbag lay. "She was lying there, on the carpet. I went over to her. She was dead. Her face was all contorted. There was a plastic bag wrapped tightly around her face and head. A plastic bag like they put over dry cleaning when they send it back. I saw it."

Dina started to step farther into the room but Lange restrained her.

"Why don't you tell us exactly what happened?" he suggested.

Dina nodded. "I was—was coming along the corridor, headed downstairs. As I started past this room— the door was shut—I heard a sound. I don't know, it was a kind of scary sound. I knew it was the room that Judith and William Justin would be occupying tonight. I knocked on the door and called out several times. When there was no answer, I tried the door-

knob. The door was unlocked. I opened it and saw—
saw her."

"You're sure she was dead?" Lange asked sharply.

"Yes." Dina nodded. "I've told you. I went over
and looked at her. She wasn't breathing. She was
dead."

"And what else did you notice?" Lange asked.
"Was her handbag there, as it is now? And the French
doors, were they open?"

"I think I noticed the bag," Dina said slowly. "I
don't remember seeing the French doors open—oh,
wait, they must have been because I could feel the
cold and I remember the wind blowing in." She nodded. "Yes, I'm sure the doors were open. I couldn't
take in everything, I was so shocked."

Lange nodded. "And then you did what?"

"I ran from the room," Dina said, "slamming the
door behind me. Then I started screaming. And you
appeared almost immediately."

"In that case," Lange said, "only a couple of minutes elapsed, three or four at the most."

Dina agreed. "I would think so, yes."

"And in that brief time," Lange said, "the body
disappeared. Which leaves us with a mystery." He
pointed to the French doors. "As I recall, they con-
nect to a terrace outside. As I further recall, the terrace connects, through other French doors, to most of
the other bedrooms on the second floor."

This time it was George who spoke. "That's correct, Lange."

Lange looked at Dina, his face grave. "You are absolutely positive Judith was dead?"

"Absolutely!" Dina answered firmly.

Lange moved them all back from the doorway and closed the door. "In that case the police must be called at once!"

Downstairs in the library, the lights—as controlled by Edward in the kitchen—flicked off and on to announce the arrival of the New Year. There was no one in the library to observe the moment.

The police were a long time in arriving at the house because of the hazardous driving conditions on the ice-slicked roads.

Lange had made the phone call to the Southampton Police, explaining the curious circumstances of the events of the evening. The first car to appear contained a police lieutenant, a sergeant, and two troopers. They all were clearly a bit skeptical that there actually had been a murder, based upon what Lange had told them in his phone call.

The lieutenant of homicide was a big man named Ralph Wainwright.

Standing apart from the others, Wainwright needled Lange briefly, saying, "You sure this isn't just a case of somebody maybe having a few too many glasses of bubbly and *thinking* they saw a dead body?"

Lange shrugged. "You couldn't prove it by me, one way or the other. It's your case."

Since the first order of business for the police was to make a search for the body, they went through Judith's bedroom carefully, looking under the bed and in the closet. Then that room was shut off for the time being while they went through the rest of the house. If they found no body inside, they would have to make a search of the grounds outside, a job no one wanted in the freezing weather.

Dina and George, their guests, and the butler and housekeeper, were asked to remain in the library with one of the troopers standing watch, while the other three policemen conducted the search. Lange was invited by Wainwright to accompany them.

The most obvious places, the other bedrooms connected to the second floor terrace, were gone through thoroughly—and fruitlessly. Next came the smaller areas, the broom closet and three linen closets located along the second floor corridor.

In the last of the three linen closets, Wainwright opened the door, drew back abruptly, grunted, and said, "Well, there she is. I'll be damned."

The body of Judith McCallum Justin lay on its side in a jackknife position. A plastic dry cleaner's bag covered the head and face, and the features of her face were distorted, eyes open and bulging from their sockets, mouth gaping open in a soundless shriek.

"Time to call in the lab guys," Wainwright said, stepping back from the linen closet and nudging the door shut with his foot.

Lieutenant Wainwright and his men were taking statements in the library, from everyone who had been in the house that evening when the other police units, the medical examiner, and the members of the foren-

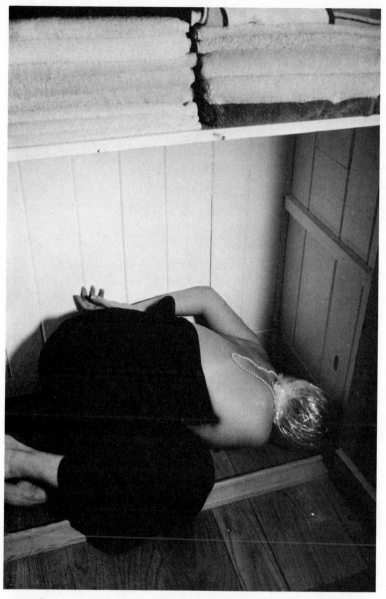

*Southampton Police photograph of the body of victim Judith McCallum Justin. Police noted strange print on shelf above body.*

31

sic unit who would conduct scientific analysis, reached the house and went to work.

Wainwright concentrated his interrogation on the whereabouts of each individual just prior to the discovery of Judith's body by Dina and just after that discovery when the body disappeared from the room. He had already determined that the body could have been removed from the room and taken by way of the outside terrace to any one of the other bedrooms and, through one of these bedrooms, to the linen closet where it was found.

According to the statements given during the interrogation, the whereabouts of certain individuals could be accounted for by certain other individuals.

Lange and Edward stated that they were together in the library not too long before the body was found. Then Lange was alone briefly but was soon again in sight of the others, as he raced upstairs almost immediately after the discovery of the body. And Edward and his wife, Julia, stated that they were together in the kitchen after Edward left the library.

Dina and George stated that they were together in their bedroom just before she left and discovered the body. As soon as Dina screamed, George hurried out of their bedroom and so was seen by Lange and others.

Valerie Carrolton and Karen McCallum stated that they were talking together in Karen's room just prior to the discovery of the body and were together in the corridor just after Dina screamed.

Arthur Carrolton was alone in his and Valerie's room just before the body was discovered, but said he too was in the corridor immediately after Dina screamed. No one could positively place him in the corridor that soon after Dina screamed, but there was a lot of confusion in the corridor at the time.

Kenneth McCallum and his brother, Evan, stated that they were in the room they were to share for the night, prior to Dina's scream, and then together in the corridor immediately afterward.

Irene Durbin stated she was in her room alone and then in the corridor. Dr. Francke stated he saw Irene in the corridor, and she stated she saw him there, although Dr. Francke could state only that he was alone in his room prior to Dina's scream.

William Justin stated that he had left Judith alone in their room earlier and then had gone to talk to Dr. Francke. Justin said Dr. Francke had not been in the room, but he had waited. When, upon hearing this statement, Dr. Francke protested vehemently that he *had* been in his room, Justin admitted he could have gone to the wrong room. This fact was made more likely since there was an empty room next to the one Dr. Francke occupied. Justin further stated he was in the corridor almost immediately after Dina screamed. No one could remember seeing Justin in the corridor.

When Justin then stated that he had bumped into Liza Parkland in the corridor and she *must* have seen him, she stated that now that she'd reconsidered, she thought she had seen him there. She stated that before she went out to the corridor, she had been alone in her room.

Once Lieutenant Wainwright had all this information, he assigned a police artist who had come with the forensic unit to make a rough sketch of the locations of the various bedrooms on the second floor. Those with doors opening onto the terrace were so marked. The artist also noted on the sketch which person or persons occupied each room.

By that time the forensic unit had completed its work.

The medical examiner gave as his preliminary opinion that Judith had been attacked from behind, the plastic dry cleaning bag forced over her head and face and wound tightly around, causing her to suffocate. A later autopsy would bear out this original opinion.

The forensic unit went over the bedroom of the victim painstakingly. A police photograph was taken of the room. The handbag found on the floor was identified as belonging to Judith Justin. Although all the contents of the handbag had been dumped on the floor, an examination of the handbag itself revealed that a small key had been concealed inside its lining. When the key was shown to the victim's husband, William Justin, and to her children, none of them could identify it nor suggest what lock it might fit.

Also found in the room were several sets of fingerprints, on a closet door and on the wall beside the light switch, next to the door to the corridor.

Before the police departed, Lieutenant Wainwright conferred privately with Lange in the hallway.

"I'd appreciate your thoughts," Wainwright said, having discovered Lange had been a homicide detective with the N.Y.P.D.

*Key found in lining of Judith McCallum Justin's handbag*

"I doubt I have any that you haven't already had." Lange paused, then added, "However, we could do a quick comparison if you'd like."

Wainwright nodded. "I would. I'll go first. The husband."

"Has to be the most likely suspect, always," Lange agreed.

"We both noticed which bedroom was closest to the linen closet where the body was found," Wainwright said.

Lange nodded. "George and Dina's. And practically everybody at the house wanted George out as president of Hitchling Health Foods. Including Judith." He looked up. "On the other hand, there's a lot of bad blood among the various diverse groups here. With one group pitted against another to gain control of the company."

"That adds up to a lot of suspects," Wainwright said. "With some more likely than others."

Lange nodded.

"Whoever did it," Wainwright said, "had to have been pretty cool and move pretty fast. To kill her, to hear the knock on the door, to hide, and then in a matter of brief minutes haul the body out, race with it across the terrace, and dump it in that linen closet, presumably while all the others were in the corridor but looking in the other direction."

"Misdirection of the eye, you might say," Lange suggested. "Another thing: You ask yourself why the body was removed from the room?"

"Sure." Wainwright held up a finger. "Either whoever killed her was looking for something and didn't find it and thought it was still on the body. "Or," he held up a second finger, "whoever killed her wanted the body to be found in that particular linen closet. To divert suspicion away—"

"Or," Lange said, "to direct it toward someone else. Misdirection of the eye again."

"Yeah," Wainwright said.

Shortly after this conversation the police left for the night.

Those remaining discussed the case for a while. Strangely enough, Dr. Francke did most of the talking, generalizing about the nature of human behavior until finally Lange drew George away from the others to ask: "Why in the world is that old character droning on and on with his opinions?"

"Wouldn't you expect it?" George asked. "After all, as I told you, he's a psychiatrist—Irene's psychiatrist."

"Her *psychiatrist*?" Lange raised his eyebrows. "When you introduced him to me, I thought you said he was her *podiatrist*. I wondered why she would have her podiatrist along with her."

George looked at Lange carefully, wondering if Lange was putting him on. Lange's face was inscrutable. George concluded Lange had a wry sense of humor.

Shortly afterward, they all retired to their rooms.

It was while George Preston and Kenneth Mc-Callum were on their way upstairs that the latter suggested he and George start making a record of notes and photographs of the case for a possible book. George liked the idea and on that early morning of the new year they began the collaboration, much of which is included in this account.

In subsequent days the police made no real progress in solving the crime. The fingerprints recovered from Judith's room were found to belong to the butler and housekeeper, to the husband, William Justin, to Dina—all of whom had reason to have left fingerprints in the room—and to Valerie Carrolton. Valerie then recalled that she had visited with Judith soon after they both arrived on New Year's Eve. No prints were found on the open French doors leading

37

*Photograph of footprint taken outside room in Southampton*

to the terrace. A single footprint from the floor of the terrace outside was recovered from the icy surface of the terrace floor.

One single, curious print was lifted from the edge of the shelf just above the body in the linen closet. Police were unable to identify precisely what it was that had left the print.

Lange had been curious about who the fourteenth guest was, the person who had been invited for New Year's Eve and had not shown up. Dina explained that the person was Virginia Andrews, a friend of hers. The bad weather had forced her to cancel the trip.

And there the case rested, awaiting further clues to its solution.

# CHAPTER TWO

(AUTHORS' NOTE: *George Preston completed a full account of the next time the group involved in this story met. Since all of the facts, as far as can be ascertained, are included in his reconstruction, his account of the events is reprinted here in his own words.*)

## A SECOND MURDER MYSTERY

*by George Preston*

It was well into the second month of the new year when most of us who had been present in Southampton at the time Judith was murdered once again found ourselves together in rather uncomfortable circumstances.

The place was Aspen, Colorado, and the reason
we all had to be there concerned the business affairs
of Hitchling Health Foods.

Before going forward with a recounting of what
transpired at Aspen perhaps I should summarize what
had taken place over the past two months since New
Year's Eve. (Note to Whomever May Publish This:
Although I have made an outline and have kept co-
pious records on the murder of Judith, I have not yet
written that story. Instead, I decided to write the full
story of the second murder while all that happened
was still fresh in my mind.)

First of all, during the past two months, there had
been changes on the board of directors of Hitchling
Health Foods. I remained as chairman with board
members Richard Durbin, Valerie and Arthur Carrolton, Evan and Kenneth McCallum, and William Justin. Justin became a new member of the board of
directors following Judith's death.

As it turned out, Judith had been quietly purchas-
ing large blocks of stock in Hitchling Health Foods
prior to her death.

According to the terms of her will, the stock went
equally to her husband, William Justin, and to her
two sons, Evan and Kenneth McCallum. The stock
was of sufficient amount that Justin had to be taken
on to the board.

Apparently Justin had been opposed to what his
late wife had been doing and they had had bitter words
about the matter while she was still alive. But once
Justin had inherited his share of the stock, he had
become actively involved in the company.

In fact it was because of Justin that we were all meeting in Aspen, Colorado. Justin was anxious to see Hitchling Health Foods merged with a holding company called Triplex, Inc. Triplex, Inc., had expressed an interest in acquiring Hitchling Health Foods.

Justin had arranged for a meeting between the board of directors and the chairman of Triplex, Inc., a man named Craig Sherwood, to discuss the possible merger. Sherwood owned a large ski lodge in Aspen and proposed we all meet there.

Here I think I should mention that ever since Judith's death, relations between Justin and Judith's two sons, Evan and Kenneth, had been quite hostile. Evan made no secret of the fact that he resented the equal inheritance Justin had received from Judith's will. Also, Evan himself was clearly ambitious and, from his actions and words since joining the board of Hitchling Health Foods, seemed determined to take over the company for himself.

Kenneth's hostility toward his stepfather went even deeper. (NOTE: Since Kenneth and I hope to collaborate on this story, with my words and his pictures, he may resent my mentioning his feelings here, but if the whole story is to be told this must be included.) In recent months, Kenneth's words to many of us had been: "I ask you, who had the most to gain from my mother's murder?" Without actually speaking William Justin's name aloud, Kenneth had made it clear whom he meant.

These then were the circumstances prior to our meeting in Aspen.

All of the board members I have named above were

to be there. In addition, Karen McCallum would be going along with her twin, Kenneth, and Evan would be bringing his fiancée, Liza Parkland. Irene Durbin and her psychiatrist-friend, Dr. Francke, would be accompanying Irene's son and daughter, Richard and Valerie, along with Richard's wife, Joanna, and Valerie's husband, Arthur.

We all flew out on a chartered plane arranged for us by Craig Sherwood—all of us, that is, except for Karen McCallum who at the last minute decided to catch a later flight. My wife, Dina, was not among us. She and I had decided she would not attend the meeting.

It was bitterly cold when we landed at the airport. Sherwood was waiting for us with a van and driver to take us to the lodge.

"I hope you revel in the snow as much as I do," Sherwood said in greeting, spreading his arms expansively to indicate the deep white drifts everywhere around us.

Craig Sherwood was well over six feet tall and looked even taller in his Cossack hat; he weighed somewhere around two hundred pounds and looked even heavier in the fur-collared windbreaker he wore. From the outset, it was clear that while Sherwood may have liked the snow, what he *really* reveled in was playing the munificent host. He had brought parkas for all of us, which he insisted we wear no matter how warmly we might already be dressed, and on the long drive to the lodge, he kept up a nonstop commentary on every peak and valley—and of course ski slope—of the landscape we passed through.

None of us, I don't think, was prepared for Sherwood's ski lodge itself. The place was no small get-away-from-it-all retreat, as one might normally expect a ski lodge to be. Instead, it was a huge complex high up on one of the mountain tops, with dozens of rooms, in the center of which was a glass-domed heated swimming pool of Olympic proportions. Lush tropical foliage flourished on the deck of the pool in the hothouse humidity of the enclosed environment. Outside the front door of the lodge, the weather was Siberian winter; outside the glass door of any bedroom, the weather was South Seas summer.

Beside the bedrooms, the lodge had an enormous dining room, a main room with a stone fireplace large enough to roast a full-grown steer in, and even a spacious conference room that could have accommodated a meeting of all the nation's mayors. The lodge was staffed by a manager, cooks, maids, butlers, cleaning personnel, and several ski instructors.

Craig Sherwood was obviously proud of the place and pleased at our astonished surprise at its opulence. Then he explained that his company, Triplex, Inc., owned the lodge and that it was one of their most successful enterprises since they rented it out for various conferences as well as to paying guests. He had, he explained, booked it solely for our use during our meeting.

"And now I suggest," Sherwood said, "we get in some skiing or, if you prefer, some swimming, and relax a bit and have some fun before we begin our business discussions."

About half the group decided to try the skiing while the other half opted for swimming.

I might say here that I really didn't feel up to either activity. I did, however, volunteer to drive to the airport and pick up Karen, who had told us about what time to expect her flight. I thought it might be beneficial to get away from the others for a while.

The lodge had a jeep which Sherwood told me to take. All the others were headed for the pool or out to the slopes when I left. I didn't expect to get lost on the way but I had a map with me in case that should happen.

It started to snow lightly as I drove away, but that didn't bother me since I had left in plenty of time to be at the airport before Karen's plane was supposed to land.

The trip would have been a simple, straightforward one except that en route I had to detour off the direct road to the airport. Some time passed before I was back on that road again. The result was that by the time I reached the airport, the plane Karen had come on had long since landed. Nor was she anywhere in sight. I made inquiries all around the airport and thus was able to ascertain that Karen had rented a car and left quite a time before.

I headed back to the lodge. This time there was no detour and I made it back much faster than I had on my trip to the airport. Even so, by the time I returned, Sherwood was anxious that we all begin our meeting; he was having the chairs arranged in the conference room, and coffee and tea brought in.

My return without Karen, nevertheless, precipitated something of a crisis. Karen was not at the lodge, nor had there been any word of her. Kenneth in particular seemed to grow very distressed over my news that I had been told at the airport she'd rented a car, yet she still hadn't reached the lodge. Sherwood sent a driver and van to look for Karen along the roads and, in a further attempt to mollify Kenneth, called the state police to report that Karen might be stranded somewhere en route to the lodge. The police said they would call back if they located her.

"And now," Sherwood said, an edge to his voice, "may we please get to our meeting."

He looked at the group milling around outside the conference room and said, exasperated, "Where's Justin? Why isn't he here?"

Liza Parkland spoke up quickly: "He was swimming when we were in the pool. We saw him go to his room." She turned to Evan. "Remember?"

Evan gave a small shrug. "I don't particularly remember," he said. "If you say so, I guess he did."

"I'll get him," I offered. "I want to drop off my parka in my room and then I'll round him up."

"Well, hurry!" Sherwood said, the impatience clear in his voice, the implication clear in the impatience that he was a man not accustomed to being kept waiting.

As I started toward my room, the other board members, Richard and Valerie and Arthur, and Evan and Kenneth entered the conference room, followed by Sherwood. Irene, Dr. Francke, Joanna, and Liza Parkland, non-board members of course, headed for the main room to wait until the meeting ended.

In my room, I hung my parka in the closet, rinsed off my face quickly in the bathroom, and then went out through the room's glass door to the pool and along the deck of the pool to Justin's room.

Looking through the glass pane of the door, it appeared the room was empty. I would have knocked on the door, but it wasn't necessary; the door stood slightly ajar. I slid it open and went inside.

It was near sundown outside by then and the only light in the room came from what was left of the sun shining down through the glass dome of the swimming pool. I brushed against an object just inside the door and would have knocked it to the floor if I hadn't caught it—a single ski pole—in time. It still appeared that the room was empty, and I was about to leave when I spotted Justin lying, asleep I guessed, on a chaise lounge.

Before I could move I thought I heard a sound outside the room on the pool deck. Although I had done nothing, at that moment I experienced an unnerving sense of fright—I suppose it could be considered natural—that I would be confronted by someone walking in through that door and catching me in the semidarkness of Justin's room.

I confess that I held my breath, waiting to hear the sound again. There was none. I moved away from the door quietly. I didn't want to make an alarming noise and startle Justin awake.

46

Later, I would ponder a thousand times or more if I hadn't made a dreadful mistake in not stepping back out through the glass door to see if there was someone there. At moments like these, one loses all sense of time passing so that later, when I would try to recall how long I was in the room, I couldn't possibly calculate whether it was only a few minutes—although I would think not more than that—or the eternity it seemed.

What I do know is that when I again thought I heard a sound outside the open glass door, I called Justin's name aloud several times and, when there was no reply, made my way to a lamp and turned it on. What I saw clearly then, for the first time, was that Justin lay on the chaise lounge—quite dead—the spike of a ski pole embedded deeply in his chest.

I'll admit I began to tremble and sweat then. Seeing the scene as it was, my instinct was to erase all traces of my presence there, turn off the light, and clear out. Let somebody else discover the body. I could always say I had knocked on the door, couldn't arouse him, and had returned to my room to look for some papers I wanted to bring to the meeting but couldn't find them; that would account for the time I had been away, out of sight of the others.

I had taken my handkerchief from my pocket and wiped away all the surfaces I had touched in the room, including the ski pole I had brushed against inside the door and almost knocked over. (I remembered how the police had gone over every inch of surface in Judith's room when she'd been murdered.) Then I realized that if there *had* been someone outside the

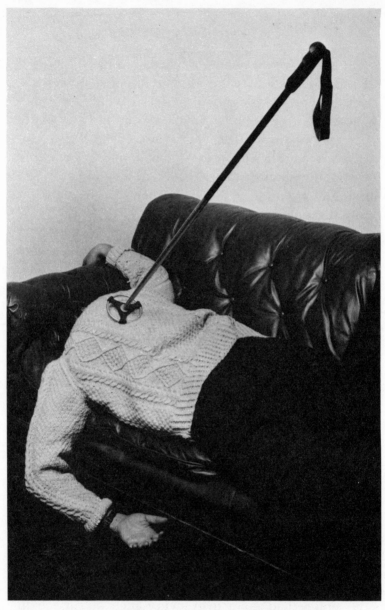

*Police photograph of body of William Justin*

glass door and if they *had* seen me in Justin's room, it would make me seem guiltier than if I related what had happened exactly as I have related it in this account.

That decided, I went quickly to the conference room and announced that Justin was dead.

There was, as would be expected, a great deal of confusion immediately afterward. Sherwood called the police and soon they were swarming all over the lodge, asking questions. They put me through a tough grilling but I stuck to my story. Meanwhile, the medical examiner and the police lab technicians were busy in Justin's room.

The police questioned the others as well, trying to find anyone who might have been out of sight long enough to go to Justin's room and kill him. There had been a couple of people who had left the conference room and returned there during my absence. Arthur Carrolton was one—he said he had gone to his and Valerie's room to get a sweater for her—and Kenneth was another.

In both cases, however, each had been seen during this time by someone else at the lodge. One of the maids had observed Arthur leave the conference room, go to his room, return with a sweater, and go back into the conference room.

I was particularly interested in Kenneth's whereabouts during the time I was away. Knowing his feelings about Justin, I suspected he might have been the person I had heard out on the pool deck after I'd first entered Justin's room. The manager of the lodge stated that he'd encountered Kenneth exiting the conference room, had lost sight of him briefly—Kenneth said he had walked toward the main room, then turned back—but had seen him using a phone just outside the conference room. (Kenneth said he'd used the phone to call the airport to try to have Karen paged, and was unsuccessful.)

Of the people waiting in the main room—Irene, Liza, Joanna, and Dr. Francke—only the doctor was absent for any period of time from the sight of the others. He claimed that he'd simply taken a stroll around the lodge. The police questioned him closely and didn't seem to be completely convinced of his activities during the period in question but, again, had no real proof of anything.

None of the people questioned, including the entire staff of the lodge, admitted to being outside Justin's room and seeing me inside. Whom then had I heard? Or was the sound I thought I'd heard simply a figment of my imagination?

Some time after, the police left, taking Justin's body with them and making it clear to all of us that they were none too pleased with the sparse results of their investigation.

We did not return to the conference room and our meeting that evening.

What occurred next was one of the most puzzling aspects of the entire experience in Aspen.

I had gone to my room to shower and change clothes for dinner, and most of the others had done so as well. Then, when I came back and was walking toward the main room, I was astonished to see Kenneth, bundled up in his parka, with his baggage around him at the front desk.

"Kenneth! Kenneth!" I called out, hurrying toward him. "Where are you going?"

It was only when I reached the desk that I found— as she slipped the hood of the parka from her head and spoke—that it was not Kenneth but his twin, Karen, standing there.

"I'm exhausted," she said. "You won't *believe* the story I have to tell."

By then all the others were in the room, all of us crowding around Karen.

And indeed, as she told her story to all of us, it was difficult to believe!

She said that the reason she'd taken a later flight than the rest of us was that she'd received a phone call in New York before the flight. The voice on the phone was disguised, a man's voice. The voice told her to fly alone to Aspen, rent a car, gave her directions of where to drive to in Aspen—and promised that if she did this and came alone, she would be given proof of who had killed her mother, Judith, and why.

Karen said she had followed instructions; she had driven to a small cabin up on the mountains between Aspen and Sherwood's lodge. When she'd reached the cabin, the front door was open. She'd called out several times, and then went in. She said she was immediately overpowered, it was too dark for her to see inside the cabin, bound, gagged, blindfolded, and earplugs put into her ears, so she could neither speak, move, see, or hear.

For the past several hours she had been held cap-

*Karen McCallum was never able to locate cabin where she said she was held. "X" marks spot she thinks was the location.*

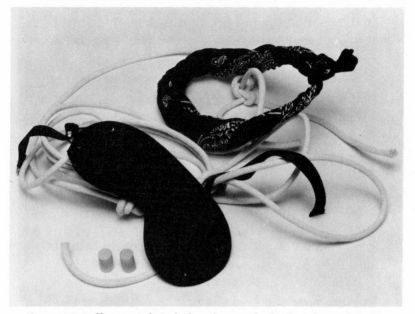

*Karen McCallum produced the above which she claimed had bound, gagged, and blindfolded her, and plugged her ears while she was held captive.*

tive like that. She had no idea whether there were one or more persons in the cabin during the time she was kept there.

Finally, she was taken from the cabin, driven a long distance in a car, removed from that car to another car, and left alone. She said her captor, or captors, had loosened the ropes around her hands after she was placed in the second car. It had taken her a while to work her hands loose, then her blindfold and gag, and to remove the earplugs.

She saw at that point that she was in the car she

had rented at the airport, her luggage undisturbed in the back seat just as she'd left it. Her car was parked on a deserted side road, the keys in the ignition.

She didn't know where she was but she started driving and finally hit a highway which, after she'd asked directions at several service stations along the way, led her here to Sherwood's lodge.

She was able to show us the ropes, the gag, the blindfold, and the earplugs she said had been used while she was a prisoner.

She was unable to supply an explanation for her odd and frightening ordeal.

The police had to be called again by Sherwood, and they came and took a statement from her.

Karen was not certain of the exact location of the cabin where she said she had been held. At the time she received the phone call in New York, she said, she had written the directions down and carried them with her to Aspen. During the time she was held helpless in the cabin, the piece of paper with the directions on it disappeared.

The following day, the police took Karen out in a patrol car to look for the cabin. Kenneth went with them. Later, they reported to us that Karen had found a cabin which she thought was the one where she'd been kept prisoner but that she couldn't be certain it was the right place. Police could find nothing inside or around the cabin, which had been abandoned for some years, to indicate it was the right place. There was no resolution to Karen's story of captivity, nor to William Justin's murder.

54

The police permitted us to leave after advising us there could be additional questioning as they continued their investigation.

We all—Craig Sherwood included—flew back east.

In subsequent days, I discussed this case with John Lange frequently. As of this writing, I know he is actively involved in trying to come up with a solution.

# CHAPTER THREE

FOLLOWING THE DEATH of William Justin in Aspen, there were several new developments in the affairs of those who are involved in this story.

Perhaps the most significant of these developments was the appearance of a newcomer to the proceedings, one Anthony Justin.

Apparently no one in the McCallum family was aware that William Justin had a son, Anthony, by his first wife who had died some years before Justin and Judith McCallum were married. This fact in itself would probably not have created any real surprise. However, when it was learned that William Justin had left a will bequeathing everything he owned—including his stock in Hitchling Health Foods—to son Anthony, there was not only surprise but bitterness as well.

Evan, Karen, and Kenneth McCallum were incensed that after their mother had left the bulk of her fortune to William Justin, he would turn around and pass that fortune on to a son who had had no connection with Judith or the McCallum family members. With his inheritance of the stock, Anthony Justin also took his place as a member of the board of directors of the company.

It's interesting to read what George Preston—who continued to keep notes on what was occurring—had to say about his first impression of Anthony Justin:

*More headaches! Today we held the first board meeting since we learned that Anthony Justin would be a new board member. Knowing in advance the feelings of antagonism on the part of Evan and Kenneth McCallum as well as a couple of others on the board to the newcomer, I had planned to try to make things go as smoothly as possible at the meeting. I must confess that Anthony Justin made that desire all but impossible!*

*There is much in him that was equally unadmirable in his late father, as well as a few unwelcome traits he has managed to develop on his own.*

*Physically, he has the same overfed, oversatisfied appearance of the elder Justin, the body and face that still have some muscle tone but will soon be turning to flab.*

*His manner, too, mimics his father; the gestures*

*mucho macho, the speech studded with tiresome ab-
breviations—"Hi," "Ya," "Fella," "Betcha," "Catch!"
meaning "do you understand?," etc.*

*On his own he seems to have mastered the ability
to not hear what anyone else is saying and to proclaim his own views on whatever the subject, as if
his was the last and deciding word.*

*Needless to say, none of this sat well with the rest
of the board—especially, as I have noted earlier, Evan
and Kenneth.*

*For myself, I foresee that my biggest problem with
him will be that he is a vocal advocate for merging
Hitchling Health Foods with Craig Sherwood's outfit
and has already begun trying to turn the other board
members to his view. I have a strong suspicion that
among the papers William Justin left before he died
was one urging Anthony to pursue this matter. Well,
I have some plans of my own to present to the board
to head off this possibility. We shall see.*

Anthony Justin had been living in San Francisco
with his fourth wife, Mitzi. He worked there as a vice
president of sales for a sporting goods manufacturer.
He quit his job after the death of his father and the
receipt of his inheritance, and he and his wife moved
to the farm they bought in Fairfield County, Connecticut.

The plan George Preston mentioned in his notes,
a plan he wanted to present to the board, was to introduce a new Health Foods product to the public.
George had been working in secret with one of the
chemists at the Hitchling Foods manufacturing plant

in Philadelphia to develop the project. It was George's hope that the new product would generate so much profit for the company that no one would want to merge with Sherwood's group.

On a morning in late March, George invited all the members of the board to the Pennsylvania plant where he would reveal the new product.

Present, in addition to George, were Richard and Valerie and Arthur Carrolton, Evan and Kenneth McCallum, and the newest member of the board, Anthony Justin. Karen McCallum, Liza Parkland, Joanna, and Justin's wife, Mitzi—although they were not members of the board—were also invited by George.

The group assembled in an anteroom of the main building, where they were all asked to don white smocks and gauze masks that covered their mouths and nostrils. There, too, George introduced them to the chief chemist, Dr. Walter Rideout, who would be conducting them through the plant.

Rideout was in his fifties—short, bald-headed, perpetually in motion. Even when standing in one spot, he'd rock back and forth on his feet, his arms and hands sweeping through the air as if orchestrating the words he spoke, mostly *fortissimo*.

Attired in smocks and masks, the group was led into the plant by Rideout. The interior of the main building was almost a city block big, a domed area brilliantly lit from above where a network of steel catwalks crisscrossed in the air high above two enormous vats of dark bubbling liquid. A dozen or so workers, also clad in white smocks and gauze masks, moved back and forth between the bubbling cauldrons.

Rideout led the group up a flight of steel-girdered stairs to the catwalk and out so that they stood overlooking one of the vats. The air was slightly hazy with a thin, powdery mist. Slipping his gauze mask down briefly, Rideout pointed to one of the vats and said: "What we need now to accomplish our project is four more of these vats. The estimated cost would be around four million dollars."

George and Rideout had considered carefully how they would make their presentation to the board members whose approval they needed: first the bad news, then the good news.

For the latter, Rideout ushered them into a glass-enclosed booth which served as his office, at the end of one of the catwalks. It was a large airy space from which the entire laboratory below could be observed. Inside here, they were able to remove their masks.

"And now," George said, "Dr. Rideout will give you a demonstration of how our proposed new product works."

At that point, Rideout walked over to an easel on which sat a large object covered by a white drop cloth. With a somewhat dramatic flourish, Rideout swept off the drop cloth to reveal a life-size photograph of a girl who must have weighed nearly two hundred pounds.

"This is a photograph of my daughter, Heather," Rideout said. "She is fifteen years old. She is the inspiration for the creation of our new product."

He picked up a jar containing a quantity of red

capsules. "The problem those who are overweight and want to reduce have is that most diet programs take too long to have any physical effect. These capsules are the answer. The individual with a weight problem who takes three of these capsules a day for ninety days will dramatically lose weight."

Rideout paused for a moment and then called out: "Heather," adding "Presto!" as a quite pretty young girl came from behind a partition, standing for a moment so all could observe her and then, blushing, turning slowly around, modeling her new figure.

There were several gasps of surprise from those observing Heather. She was svelte and shapely, a real knockout, her weight a good one hundred pounds lighter than in the photograph on the easel.

"And this transformation took only three months," Rideout said. "What's more, the pills are safe—even healthy—to take. We have already received clearance from the F.D.A. to manufacture and sell them."

There was applause from most of the group in the office.

George said: "We plan to call the product 'Trim-Safe.' We believe it will make a fortune for Hitchling Health Foods. We are ready to go into full production. But we do need the additional vats to supply the demand we expect."

There were enthusiastic responses from all around the room.

George, beaming, added, "And now we will all retire to the conference room where there is chilled champagne waiting."

Fixing their masks back in place, they filed out of the glass-enclosed booth after Dr. Rideout and Heather. Down below, most of the workers were leaving the floor for their lunch break.

Glasses and buckets of chilled champagne were on the table in the conference room as they entered, several of the group stopping off en route to visit the washrooms.

George poured champagne as the group finally began to gather around the conference table. Having shed their masks and smocks, they all began to animatedly discuss the new product.

As George passed filled glasses of champagne around the table, he suddenly paused, noting that Rideout, Arthur Carrolton, and Anthony Justin were still missing.

When he inquired about them, he was told, in turn, by Valerie that Arthur had discovered his gold pen was missing and had gone to retrace his steps to see if he could find it; by Mitzi Justin that her husband, Anthony, had said he was going to the washroom and that that was the last she had seen of him; and by Heather Rideout that her father had remembered he'd left the written formula for "Trim-Safe" behind in the glass-enclosed booth and had gone to retrieve it.

"Now that I think of it," Valerie said, "Arthur has been away for a good while."

"I think I'd better take a look," George said.

The others remained in the conference room, sipping champagne. Ten, perhaps fifteen, minutes passed before one of the security guards came rushing into

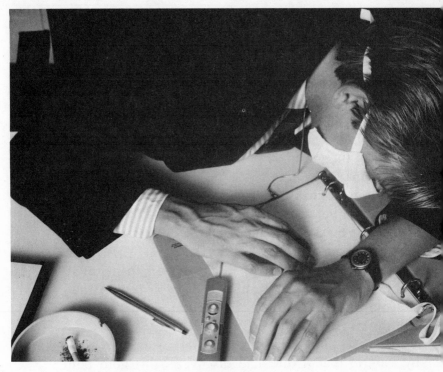

*Police photograph of body of Arthur Carrolton in office of Hitchling Health Foods plant*

the room, saying that Mr. Preston had asked that all of them please come at once to the glass-enclosed booth.

Liza Parkland stayed behind in the conference room with Heather Rideout, since none of them knew what might have happened.

When the rest of the group reached the booth, George was standing in the doorway, his face grim. "There's been a terrible tragedy," he said.

Dr. Rideout and Anthony Justin joined the group just as George made his announcement.

"It's Arthur," George said. "He—he's dead. I've already called the police."

Valerie collapsed when she heard George's words, and was helped away by Mitzi Justin.

The story George told them (and later told the police) was that on reaching the glass-enclosed booth minutes earlier he had found Arthur Carrolton slumped forward across the desk. On the desk was the open notebook left by Rideout with the formula for the new product, "Trim-Safe," in it. A small Minox camera hung by a strap from Arthur's neck.

A short while later when the police arrived, they declared—after an examination of the body and the office—that Arthur apparently was strangled by some unknown object applied to his throat with considerable force. This fact was later verified by an autopsy.

Police theorized from what they observed of the office that Arthur Carrolton had been photographing the formula with the Minox camera when he was attacked from behind, a snare-like object forced over his head and around his throat, and strangled to death. The police were never able to discover what object was used in the murder.

One of the laboratory's security guards stated that not long before the time the murder must have been committed he had been headed toward the booth, on the catwalk. While he was still some distance away, the guard stated, he had seen a person in white smock and gauze mask exit the glass booth. The guard was too far away to be able to identify the person, and at the time paid little attention to the incident. From this statement the police again theorized that whoever killed Arthur Carrolton probably spotted the guard and left hurriedly.

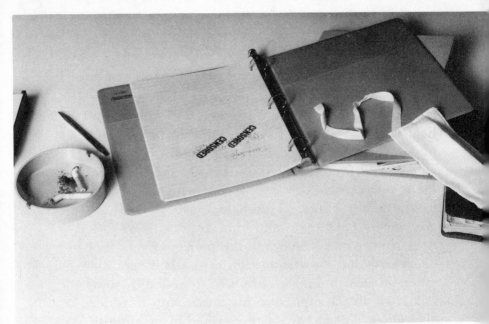

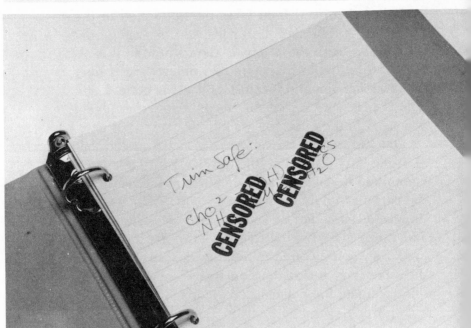

*These photos were developed from film found inside Minox camera which was slung around the neck of dead Arthur Carrolton. The black strips blocking out the formula symbols were put in before publication here.*

Since George Preston, Dr. Rideout, and Anthony Justin were out of sight of the others prior to the moment Arthur's body was found, they were questioned at great length by the police.

George's explanation of his whereabouts was the same as he had given earlier: that he went directly from the conference room to the glass-enclosed booth and found Arthur dead. Dr. Rideout stated that although he had left the conference room to retrieve his notebook with the formula in it, he had made a short detour to check on an experiment being made in another area of the plant. When he had finally arrived at the glass-enclosed booth, the others were already there. Unfortunately, Rideout could not produce anyone who had seen him in the other area of the plant since all the workers were on their lunch hour. Anthony Justin, for his part, declared he had been in the washroom during the whole time he was absent from the conference room; he had then emerged from the washroom to see all the others up on the catwalk and had hurried to join them.

Police were curious about what the film in the Minox camera would show. Later, when the film was developed, they were unable to find any further clues as to whom the killer might be, nor of the object used to kill Arthur. (AUTHORS' NOTE: Copies of all the photographs developed from the film in the Minox camera are included in this chapter.)

Valerie Carrolton became virtually obsessed with her husband's murder and swore she would uncover his killer and get revenge.

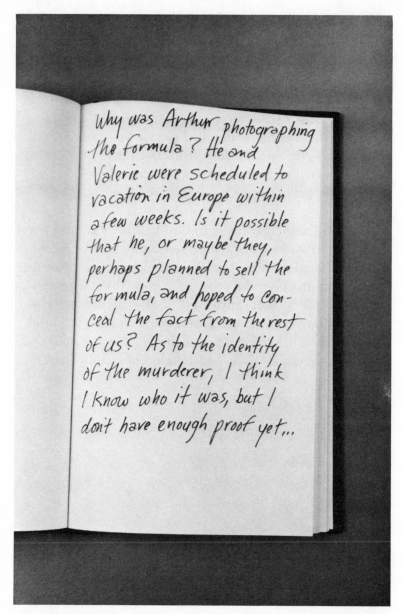

*A photograph reproduction of George Preston's handwritten notes*

And later, George Preston would record in his notes: *Why was Arthur photographing the formula? He and Valerie were scheduled to vacation in Europe within a few weeks. Is it possible that he, or maybe they, perhaps planned to sell the formula, and hoped to conceal the fact from the rest of us? As to the identity of the murderer, I think I know who it was, but I don't have enough proof—yet.*

John Lange always regretted that he was not present when Arthur Carrolton was killed, since he believed he might have found some evidence at the time to help him solve the case. Still, now that there were two murders that appeared to be somehow connected, he was following the events closely, although he did not have access until much later to many of the photographs taken—and included in this chapter.

# CHAPTER FOUR

(AUTHORS' NOTE: *George Preston and his wife, Dina, were vacationing on the Riviera a few weeks after the murder of Arthur Carrolton at the Hitchling plant in Pennsylvania, when George received the memo that follows. The authors of the present work decided to reproduce the actual memo sent to George, which also has some of George's own comments written in the margins. Once again, Kenneth McCallum obtained the photographs that the authors felt were pertinent to the facts contained in the memo.)*

TO:        George Preston

FROM:      John Lange

SUBJECT:   Confidential Investigation

As you requested in your phone call, I have conducted an
intensive investigation into: 1) the mysterious death of
Craig Sherwood of TRIPLEX, Inc. and: 2) the equally
mysterious disappearance of Valerie Carrolton, both of which
occurred during your recent absence.

*Some-*
*Yes!*

Some of the facts are no doubt already known to you, through
stories in the media, but I would like you to have a full
account of what I have learned.

First, Sherwood: his body was found submerged under a
couple of feet of water in an overflowing shower stall in
the bathroom of his Manhattan townhouse.  The body was
discovered by Craig's manservant, one Timothy Grimes on the
morning of April 26.

*get*
*back-*
*ground*
*on him*
*!!!*

Grimes, who had been employed by Sherwood for approximately
ten years, did not live in the house.  He did have his own
key to the townhouse but in his statement to the police,
Grimes said the front door to the house was open when he
arrived, and made his gruesome discovery.  He immediately
dialed the 911 police emergency number.

*Can you*
*be sure*

Grimes left everything in the bathroom untouched until the
police arrived.

The police report that the body was lying on its back in the
shower stall under water, the shower still beating down full
force and the water collecting to a depth of a couple of
feet behind the closed glass doors of the shower before it
overflowed into the bathroom itself and out into the hall.
The body lay in such a position that it effectively blocked
the drain and allowed the water to collect inside.  A later
examination of the body revealed a deep gash in the back of

*?!!!*

the skull.  Although the police could not positively fix the
cause of the gash in the back of the skull, there was a
towel rack in the back of the shower, attached to the wall,
an edge of which could have caused the gash if Sherwood had
slipped in the shower and hit the back of his head against
it.  If this is what happened, police have theorized that
Sherwood could then have fallen, unconscious, to the floor
of the shower, his body blocking the drain and thus have
drowned - death by drowning being the official verdict of
the medical examiner.  (The spray from the shower would have
washed away any traces of blood on the towel rack.)

I would think not!

The police did not rule out the possibility that Sherwood was knocked in the head and dumped into the shower. In which case, they did note, it would have taken at least two people to have moved the body and placed it in the shower.

One curious note is that in the livingroom police found some spilled powder - later analyzed as face powder - on the floor and in it was a print of an object still not identified.

Can this be followed up?

In any event, police did make an investigation into all of Craig Sherwood's activities on the day and night before the body was discovered (the police were particularly interested in this time period because the autopsy showed he had died sometime during the night before the morning of April 26).

Understatement!

It was this police investigation that brought into the case the names of several individuals connected to Hitchling Health Foods, a circumstance I know concerns you.

What has been verified is that Craig Sherwood arrived in Manhattan only one day earlier, April 25, before he died. He flew in from Colorado early that day. Timothy Grimes had been sent a day earlier than that to have the house ready for Sherwood.

Any other phone calls?

As far as can be ascertained Sherwood did not leave the townhouse from the time he arrived until he died. He was, nevertheless, busy throughout that day. On the telephone. And almost all his calls were made to members of the board of directors of Hitchling Foods.

It has been established that that day he made telephone calls to, in no particular sequence, Richard and Joanna Durbin, Evan and Kenneth McCallum, and Anthony Justin.

Each of these stated to police that they had received phone calls from Sherwood. In addition, although Valerie Carrolton was never located again after the time Sherwood was found dead, others stated that Valerie had talked to them over the phone that day and had discussed the strange call she, too, had had from Sherwood.

In each call Sherwood made, the message was the same: it was of the utmost importance that they meet with him at his townhouse that evening after 8 PM to discuss a matter crucial to the survival of Hitchling Health Foods.

*Police were unable to identify this impression found in spilled powder in Craig Sherwood's town house.*

(As you know, your secretary reported that you, too, received such a call at your office in New York from Sherwood. She also has stated that he seemed extremely agitated to learn that you were out of the country and left a message for you to call him upon your return.)

*Did not reciere message*

The responses of the various individuals contacted by Sherwood were, according to their accounts, varied.

Kenneth McCallum stated he was not interested in what Sherwood might have to say, and did not go to Sherwood's house.

Evan McCallum claims Sherwood never reached him, so he knew nothing of the proposed meeting. He was in Pennsylvania all day and evening.

*Can we verify this???*

Anthony Justin told police that he and his wife had tickets for the theatre and so he went to Sherwood's earlier, around 7 PM. Justin says he and Sherwood talked and then Justin left. (According to Justin, what Sherwood wanted to talk about was the merger of Hitchling Health Foods and Triplex, Sherwood claiming that if the board of directors of Hitchling did not act promptly, the merger offer would fall through.)

*Sneaky business !!! ...*

For the record: there is no one to substantiate who did or did not visit Sherwood that evening; Timothy Grimes has said Sherwood told him he could leave at 6 PM, and he did.

*Baloney*

*Again— can we verify?*

Richard and Joanna Durbin admit they were curious to hear what Sherwood had to say but that they were unable to get by to see him until close to 10 PM. They say they rang the bell and knocked on the door of the house but there was no answer. They say all the lights in the house were off and it never occurred to them to try the door and see if it was unlocked.

Finally, there is the matter of Valeria Carrolton. That day, the 25th, she made several phone calls to other members of the board and to her mother, Irene. They report that she seemed puzzled by Sherwood's phone call, but that she said she would try to attend the meeting, although she told Anthony Justin and her brother, Richard, that she would probably be about an hour late.

*What is Valerie up to?*

Now we come to the time period between when Justin has stated he left the house and Richard and Joanna say they arrived. When police questioned neighbors along Sherwood's block to find out what they might have heard or seen that evening, the people who live in the townhouse next to

*What are the names of these neighbors?*

*Anthony Justin produced ticket stubs to show he had been at theater with his wife the night Craig Sherwood died.*

*Unidentified fingerprints found on a glass in Craig Sherwood's town house*

*Might be important*

Sherwood's stated that somewhere between 8:30 and 9 PM, a woman rang their doorbell and asked if the place was the residence of Craig Sherwood. They directed her to Sherwood's house. Their description of the woman to the police was, at best, vague. The woman was hot too tall, was wearing dark glasses, a scarf over her head and a coat with a turned-up collar. Her hair, they said, was dark. That's about it, as far as Sherwood's death is concerned. Of course the police dusted the house for prints. One set matched up with Justin's prints and the rest were eliminated except for two sets that still remain unidentified. Some of the prints were lifted from cocktail glasses found in the livingroom. Since Justin stated he and Sherwood had a drink, his prints were to be expected. The autopsy showed that Sherwood had traces of alcohol in his bloodstream but not of sufficient quantity to cause drunkenness.

*!!!*

As you know, following Sherwood's death, it was discovered that he had siphoned off money from TRIPLEX, Inc. and bought most of the outstanding stock in Hitchling Health Foods. The speculation is that once the merger went through, he planned to sell off the Hitchling stock at a high premium and make a killing for himself, which would explain why he was pressing so hard for the merger.

It would appear he only had a limited time to return to TRIPLEX, Inc. the money he had surreptitiously taken. (There is the possibility that Sherwood may have tried to influence one or more members of the Hitchling board to push the merger through.)

*They should!*

The police, having come into possession of the above information, in addition to the curious manner of Sherwood's death, naturally had questions about the case. And, naturally, one of the persons they very much wanted to question was the missing Valerie Carrolton. The put out an A.P.B. on her but, as of now, she hasn't been found.

Now, 2) the background of the disappearance of Valerie Carrolton.

As you already know, she became somewhat irrational almost immediately after the murder of her husband, Arthur. She went about everywhere announcing that she positively knew who had killed him. But she would never name a name. I personally spoke with her on several occasions. Each time she declared that she knew the identity of the killer but she would not reveal who she thought it was, nor why. I cautioned her that it was unwise to make such statements but my words apparently did little good.

Then, within ten days to two weeks before the death of Craig Sherwood and her disappearance, she claimed that on three separate occasions someone had tried to kill her; once when she was coming home late in the evening and, so she said, a car tried to run her down; again, so she said, when someone tried to attack her on the street as she was returning home and; another time when, so she said, someone tried to break into her apartment. There were no witnesses, no evidence, to support any of these incidents. Frankly, I do not know what to make of them. The last time she was seen was on the night of April 25. The doorman at her apartment building has said he put her into a taxicab at approximately 8 PM. After it was discovered she was missing, on April 26, members of her family, including her mother, Irene, went to her apartment. They have said that as far as they could tell, none of her clothing or luggage was missing. If she disappeared voluntarily, she took nothing with her, as far as anyone has been able to ascertain.

There is, finally, one puzzling postscript concerning Valerie Carrolton: when I questioned the doormen in her building (tipping them generously for the information) they told me that several times in the days just before she disappeared, she was visited by a man none of them had ever seen before - or have ever seen since she disappeared. They didn't know who he was but they described him as short and stocky and about my age. I have no idea whether or not he is of importance in the case but I intend to keep him in mind.

I shall of course continue my investigation of all of the above and will keep you advised.

*I want the name of this man!*

# CHAPTER FIVE

SOON AFTER GEORGE Preston received the memo from John Lange, as recounted in the previous chapter, the board of directors of Hitchling Health Foods was scheduled to hold a full board meeting in London. Arrangements for the meeting had been made some months earlier. The purpose of the meeting was to discuss with members of the London office the expansion of Hitchling Health Foods operations in England.

Despite the recent deaths, murders, and disappearances of various individuals connected to the company, George Preston saw no reason to change the plans for the meeting. He and Dina flew from the Riviera to London to join the others arriving from the United States.

The company had booked accommodations and a conference room for the first weekend in March at one of London's finest hotels, Cantrey House, on Park Lane. There, George and Dina joined Richard and Joanna Durbin, Evan, Kenneth, and Karen Mc-Callum, Anthony Justin and his wife, Mitzi, and Irene Durbin and her friend Dr. Francke. Although these last two were not members of the board, they had accompanied Irene's son and daughter-in-law—Richard and Joanna—on the trip. In addition, Liza Parkland had been brought along by Evan Mc-Callum.

Naturally, much of the discussion among them when they all met for the first time centered upon the disappearance of Valerie, Irene's daughter, and the death of Craig Sherwood.

They were all housed on the hotel's third floor, and they had met for drinks in George and Dina's suite.

"I'm terribly worried about what might have happened to poor Valerie," Irene said, shaking her head. Dr. Francke held her hand, trying to comfort her.

George told them all about the memo he'd received from Lange, adding, "He's as baffled as the rest of us. However, he does have one small lead—I really can't say more than that about it—which he's following up."

"Surely no one believes she had anything to do with the death of that Sherwood person," Irene said, looking around the room. "I understand the police sent out some kind of *wanted* notice on her."

"An All Points Bulletin," George said. "Lange mentioned it in his memo. What they want her for is questioning, that's all."

"She *was* awfully distraught before she vanished," Anthony Justin said.

"So would you be, too," Irene snapped back angrily, "if your—your spouse had been murdered!"

"Please," Justin said, raising his hands in the air. "I didn't mean to imply—"

"Then don't!" Irene snapped again.

George interceded, smoothing the ruffled feelings of each, and soon afterward the group separated.

They had dinner together that evening in the hotel's dining room. Outside torrential rains were falling, weather which was to continue throughout the weekend and to keep them all more or less confined to the hotel.

Attending the dinner that evening were three officers of Hitchling Foods' London branch. The three were Llewellyn Jamison, manager of the office; Helen Maury, chief accountant; and Robert Bixler, vice president in charge of sales.

Jamison was a quiet, soft-spoken man, suited by Savile Row. Throughout dinner he had everyone else at the table at a slight disadvantage since wherever he directed his attention, the light from the room's chandelier reflected blindingly off his bald pate and the half-glasses he wore well down on his nose.

Helen Maury was a spinsterish-looking (that appearance accurate to her marital status), fat, fortyish woman. She had a quick, sharp mind and let you know what was on it with a tongue equally quick and cutting.

Robert Bixler was burly, jovial, reddish-haired, with a brush moustache.

Most of the conversation at the table was small talk and generalized, exchanges straight out of the media on both sides of the Atlantic. The Hitchling Foods discussions were held for the meeting of the board the next day.

During the whole course of the dinner the group was distracted by the commotion taking place in the rest of the dining room. There was a group of some one hundred persons holding another kind of gathering.

George Preston hadn't known about this other affair when he'd booked accommodations at the hotel, and he'd been dismayed to find out about it when he, Dina, and the others arrived. By then it was too late to change to another hotel and so they had stayed, none too pleased.

As it turned out, on this particular Friday, Saturday, and Sunday, the hotel was holding a so-called Murder Mystery Weekend, the kind of event that has recently become popular in parts of England, the United States, and Canada. At these various Murder Mystery Weekends, the hotels provide—for a fee— rooms, meals, and a mystery which participating guests try to solve for prizes and for the fun of solving the mystery.

Most of the Hitchling Foods group thought it ironic to find themselves in the midst of a fictional murder plot after having been involved personally in real murder plots. "There's no escaping the damn subject wherever we go," George had complained.

But Karen McCallum had said she thought it was great fun to be around and watch while the guests of the Mystery Weekend went about the hotel attempting to solve whatever fictional crime was to unfold, even though none of the group would participate.

It was Karen who got all the details about this particular plot from the hotel's manager.

The concept for this hotel's mystery plot was rather more elaborate than that conceived for the usual Mystery Weekend. As the manager explained to Karen, at most Mystery Weekends, guests who have signed up to participate are given various roles to play during the proceedings, according to the scenario that has been written. (In all such Mystery Weekends there are also of course professional actors involved who move the plot along and explain it, according to the script.)

One difference this weekend, the manager explained to Karen, was that as the participants first arrived at the hotel, they were given individual rubber face masks and wigs which they had to wear from then on for the three days they'd be there. For instance, one of the female guests was given upon arrival a face mask of an old woman and a wig of long gray hair, and was told that she was to be a "Countess Irina"; a male guest was presented with a face mask of a sinister-looking, swarthy Russian and a wig of thick black hair, and was told he was a "Boris Chekovitch"—a spy—and so on.

The plot was to take place on an ocean liner en route from France to the United States and the time was to be in the early 1930s. Because the setting was an ocean liner all those involved in the mystery had rooms on the second floor and would use the hotel's first floor dining room as if it were the ship's dining room. The ship was the S.S. *Van Dyne.*

As the weekend progressed, the mystery plot would develop, a plot that had to do with a murder or murders occurring among the shipload of passengers. Everything taking place would have a 1930s flavor.

While the Hitchling Foods group was dining, a small band in the room (now the ship's band) was playing a medley of tunes: "On the Sunny Side of the Street," "Exactly Like You," "Just One More Chance," "Lazy River," "Night and Day." The guests of the Mystery Weekend danced in their masks and wigs.

George Preston nodded toward the bandstand. "I'll say one thing; they don't write songs like that anymore."

"Watching them dance," Kenneth McCallum said, "it's a bit eerie, in their masks I mean. Never a change of expression."

"Makes you wonder what some of them might look like under the masks, eh?" Bixler said.

"Of course," Dr. Francke put in, "underneath, they're wearing another mask. Just as we all wear masks every day to conceal ourselves from others."

Soon after, the Hitchling Foods group finished dinner. Jamison, Maury, and Bixler left the hotel until the next day, and the others went up to their rooms and to bed. Throughout that night, there were odd sounds—shouts, laughter, once something that sounded like a muffled gunshot—from the floor below as the mystery plot unfolded.

The next day was dark and dismal, rain falling without letup. The board members assembled in the conference room for a meeting with the three members of the London office. They discussed increasing the staff of the office, especially in the sales department. George Preston was anxious to build a larger staff in anticipation of the increased business he believed Hitchling Foods would do with its new product, "Trim-Safe." He did not, however, tell the Londoners about the product. He and the other members of the board wanted to keep the new product secret until it was introduced on the market.

The group met throughout the day, taking a break from time to time for lunch, tea, drinks, and dinner. During each of the breaks they would be joined by the others who had come over from the States. Karen made a point of appearing to give a breathless report on the progress of the Mystery Weekend plot.

At lunch she told the group: "It's really neat what's happening. See, the way they're doing it is that the people who are supposed to be on the ocean liner are a strange mixture, like the characters who collected in Rick's Place in the movie *Casablanca*. The murder hasn't taken place yet. Last night there was a shot fired at the Russian, but it missed."

At tea time Karen's report was: "Now the Russian has disappeared and everybody's trying to figure out if he was pushed overboard or what. And who was after him and why."

At dinner Karen joined the group to say: "Now it turns out that the Russian wasn't who he seemed to be. According to the plot of the mystery he was really a famous detective named Hector Pirouette. The Russian outfit was just a disguise. They say he was after some unknown person on board. But now he's missing."

That night again there were strange emanations from the lower floors of the hotel as the Mystery Weekend plot continued. From time to time during the early hours of the morning, one or another of the Hitchling group awoke to hear voices, shouts, and what sounded like furniture being overturned.

At breakfast in the hotel dining room the following day—Sunday—the last day the Hitchling Foods group would be in London, George complained, "I can't say this has been a particularly restful weekend, what with all the disturbances that have been going on."

"Oh, George," Karen said, laughing, "you're just an old grouch. Trying to figure out the plot has been fun, and today it ends."

Scarcely had she spoken the words than all the participants in the Mystery Weekend came trooping into the dining room, where they were addressed by the hotel's manager.

"Listen!" Karen said to those at her table.

"Ladies and gentlemen," the manager said, "all you would-be sleuths, our mystery aboard the good

ship S.S. *Van Dyne* is about to end. By now you should
have collected enough clues to guess the answer to
our mystery. Please fill out the cards you'll find on
the tables in front of you. If any of you have the correct solution, we'll award out prizes."

While those who were involved in the game began to write out their answers, Karen said, "I bet I
know the solution. Do you want to hear it?"

"Oh, Karen," her twin, Kenneth, said, "nobody here
except you cares about that silly business—"

"On the contrary, Karen," Dina said, "tell us what
you think it is."

Karen looked around the table mischievously. "I
think it's going to turn out that the person they call
Hector Pirouette isn't overboard or dead at all. Since
the ship is about to dock, he'll suddenly appear and
shed his Russian disguise to reveal he's the detective. But, but"—she said hurriedly—"the solution is
that the detective outfit is just another disguise and
that really he's, remember this is supposed to be the
1930s, that he's really Adolf Hitler sneaking into the
United States to spy on the country, in preparation
for World War II. And somebody on board is trying
to kill him."

All of them at the table broke into laughter. Dina
clapped her hands and cried, "Bravo, Karen! If that's
not the answer, it should be."

While they were still laughing, a man in the Mystery Weekend party rose suddenly and ran to one of
the windows, shouting: "Man overboard! Man overboard! I see him! It's Hector Pirouette!"

The man who had run to the window looked out and then turned, *real* terror in his voice, as he shouted, "Oh my God! There really is a body down there! A real body lying in the rain!"

As most of the people in the room started to stand, the hotel manager spoke up loudly and firmly: "Please keep your seats! Stay where you are until we see what this is all about."

He then hurried to the window, looked out, and turned, his face ashen, to say: "There is a body lying down there. This is not a part of the Mystery Weekend, I assure you. Please, everyone remain here until I've summoned the police!"

There was a sudden ominous silence around the table where the Hitchling Foods group sat and then George Preston said solemnly, "Oh, no! I have a terrible feeling." He looked around the table. "Has anyone seen Evan this morning?" He turned toward Liza Parkland.

"I thought he was probably sleeping late," she said. "I haven't seen him since last night."

George stood up abruptly and hurried to the window. He stood looking down from the window for a long time before slowly returning to the table.

"Is it—?" Liza asked fearfully.

George nodded. "I'm afraid so. From what I could see, it looks like him. The hotel manager and a couple of other people are already down there. I imagine the police will be along shortly. This is terrible."

No one else spoke for a while. Several uniformed bobbies soon arrived, accompanied by a couple of men in plainclothes and the hotel manager.

The hotel manager and one of the men in plainclothes came directly to George Preston.

The hotel manager spoke. "Mr. Preston, I'm sorry to inform you but the dead man appears to have been one of the members of your group."

George nodded. "I looked from the window."

"Mr. Evan McCallum," the hotel manager said.

George nodded again.

The man in plainclothes said, "I'm Inspector Hoskins, New Scotland Yard. It appears the dead man either fell or was pushed from an upper floor window. I'm afraid I'll have to ask all of you some questions."

The inspector then turned, indicating the other gathering in the room, asking curiously, "Who are they? And what in the world are they all doing in those odd-looking outfits and those masks they're wearing?"

The hotel manager explained about the Mystery Weekend.

"Well, damn it," the inspector said impatiently, "I want all of them unmasked right now. We'll have questions of them as well, and I want to be able to see their faces when they answer."

Inspector Hoskins then turned his attention back to the table where George Preston sat, and began writing down information about Evan McCallum and the other Americans in the group. When he had finished, he asked, "Do any of you have reason to suspect that Mr. Evan McCallum might have been a victim of foul play?"

Before anyone at the table could reply, there was

a startled outcry from Karen. She had been observing the other group in the room as they unmasked. When she caught sight of one of the people who had just removed a mask, she was unable to stifle her outcry.

"Look! Look!" Karen said shrilly. "It's—it's Valerie—Valerie Carrolton!"

"Valerie!" Irene cried, overturning her chair in the excitement and hurrying over to her previously missing daughter.

The others at the table sat in stunned silence, not knowing what to think and simply waiting until Irene brought Valerie back to them.

Inspector Hoskins, exasperated, said, "Will someone kindly tell me what's going on?"

Valerie, although she was trembling, said, "I will. I'll tell you everything. It's a long story."

During the next several hours, the police established several facts: The man who had run to the window shouting "Man overboard!" and who had spotted the real body lying below, admitted sheepishly that he had done it as a gag. In other words, it had been a simple coincidence—and not a part of the Mystery Weekend plot—that he was the one who saw the body first.

In addition, the police established that Evan McCallum's body lay in an areaway directly under a window in the third floor room he had occupied, Room 329. He had died of a broken neck, caused by the fall.

As for Valerie Carrolton, she told her story in Dina

*The mask and wig worn by Valerie Carrolton during the Mystery Weekend at hotel in London*

91

and George's suite, with all of the others there: Richard and Joanna, Irene and Dr. Francke, Kenneth and Karen, Anthony and Mitzi Justin, Liza Parkland, George and Dina. Inspector Hoskins paced up and down as Valerie talked, while one of Hoskins's men, Sergeant Conners, took down in shorthand everything she said.

"I mentioned earlier," Valerie said, "that it's a long story."

It had all begun several weeks earlier, Valerie told them, when her husband, Arthur, was murdered in the Hitchling plant in Pennsylvania.

"I was convinced I knew who the murderer was," Valerie said. "But I didn't know why. I did make a big mistake, though; I announced that I thought I knew who the murderer was."

She said then that someone tried to kill her. She was frightened. And nobody seemed to believe her. During this period, she added, she hired a private detective to check on the man she believed to be her husband's killer and to check on some of the others who were present in the laboratory that day.

"To my astonishment," Valerie said, "the detective—his name is Joe Pinnero, and he'll verify what I'm telling you—found out that Liza Parkland worked for Craig Sherwood at Triplex, Inc., before she became involved with Evan McCallum. Do you see what I'm getting at?"

"Frankly, no," Liza Parkland said indignantly. "It was never any big secret that I once worked for Triplex, Inc."

"It was a secret to me," Valerie said.

"I believe you're making this whole thing up, about the private detective, to attempt to explain away something else you haven't told us about. In fact, I believe you knew about my association with Craig Sherwood all along. I made no secret of it—" Liza Parkland paused and glanced around the room.

"Actually," Anthony Justin said, "I knew it. I don't know whether I heard it from you or from Evan."

Inspector Hoskins interrupted. "In any event, Mrs. Carrolton, what is your point?"

Valerie took a deep breath before she continued. Everybody knew Sherwood was trying to push through a merger of Triplex, Inc., and Hitchling Foods. When she, Valerie, found out Liza had worked for Sherwood and Triplex, she then suspected that Sherwood and Evan were in on a plot together to push the merger through, each man making a fat profit, and that Liza Parkland was the go-between.

"When I received the phone call from Sherwood in New York about a meeting at his town house," she said, "I decided to go." Here her voice dropped low. "I did. When I got to his house that evening, no one answered the door. I went inside. There was no one there. I heard water running upstairs. I went up. He was in the shower, dead. I panicked and ran. I thought somebody was trying to set me up. I still think so. That they were either going to kill me, as they'd tried to do, or frame me for murder."

"And exactly who was it," Inspector Hoskins asked, "that you believed had killed your husband?"

Valerie explained that she believed Evan had killed her husband in the Hitchling plant in Pennsylvania. What she suspected was that it was *Evan* who had been photographing the formula for "Trim-Safe" when Arthur walked in on him. Then Evan had somehow strangled Arthur and placed him in the chair at the desk, to make it appear *Arthur* had been photographing the formula. Evan had had to do this, Valerie added, because one of the guards was approaching and he didn't have time to do anything else. So he left even the camera and film inside the camera, which he slung around Arthur's neck.

"The reason Evan was photographing the formula," Valerie went on, "was that he and Sherwood wanted to pass it on to some other company and let them bring it out ahead of Hitchling Foods. Otherwise, if Hitchling Foods made a success of the new product, as the company will, there'd be no chance of a merger. Meanwhile, Sherwood would have no chance to repay the money he'd taken from Triplex quickly enough."

"And when you disappeared," Inspector Hoskins asked again, "where were you?"

"Here," Valerie said. "In this hotel. I knew there was supposed to be a Hitchling board meeting here this weekend. So I came early and checked in under an assumed name. *Then* I discovered there was to be a Mystery Weekend and how it was to work. So I joined in. Wearing a costume and mask provided me with a perfect disguise."

"And why did you want to be here?" the inspector inquired. "And in disguise?"

"I wanted to throw a scare into Evan," Valerie said. "I wanted him to know someone knew he had killed Arthur."

What she did, she said, was type out a note, saying, quote: I KNOW YOU KILLED ARTHUR AND WHY. I KNOW THAT LIZA PARKLAND WORKED FOR CRAIG SHERWOOD AND TRIPLEX, AND THAT YOU AND SHE AND SHERWOOD WERE WORKING TO FORCE A MERGER BETWEEN TRIPLEX AND HITCHLING FOODS, FOR YOUR PERSONAL GAIN, unquote. She left the note unsigned.

"Last night I slipped the note under the door of Evan's room," Valerie said. "I hoped to scare him into—well, something that would give him away. That's all I did. I didn't see him. I didn't push him out the window," she added, concluding her statement.

Later, when police went to Evan's room, they found it undisturbed but with the window pushed open to the top.

They were unable to locate the note Valerie said she'd written, either in the room or on the body of Evan McCallum.

Toward the end of that day George Preston received an air mail letter from John Lange, from New York. It contained a note and a newspaper clipping.

The note was tersely written. It stated that Lange thought he had uncovered the identity of the man rumored to have visited Valerie Carrolton in the days before she disappeared. The note explained that one of the doormen in Valerie's building who had been questioned by Lange had kept Lange's personal card and had mailed him a newspaper clipping which included a man's photograph. The doorman thought he

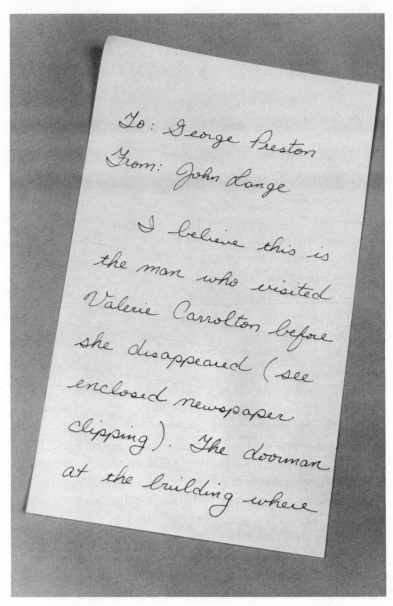

*Copy of note sent by John Lange to George Preston*

# PRIVATE EYE FOUND SHOT TO DEATH

Private Investigator Joseph Pinnero was found shot to death in his Manhattan office yesterday. Police believe the death was an accident.

According to a spokesman for the Manhattan South Precinct, Pinnero's body was discovered by a cleaning woman working in the building, who notified police.

Officers arriving on the scene stated that the private eye was slumped over in a chair behind his desk, a gun—later established as belonging to him—in his hand.

Police are of the opinion that Joseph Pinnero was cleaning the revolver at the time it accidentally discharged, fatally wounding him.

Although officials have not ruled out possible homicide, they say there is no evidence of foul play.

*Copy of newspaper clipping and photograph of Joseph Pinnero sent by John Lange to George Preston*

*Interior of hotel room in London occupied by Evan McCallum just before his death*

recognized the photograph; it was the same man who had visited Valerie. By the time Lange received the clipping, it was over a week old.

The newspaper story reported that a Manhattan private detective, Joseph Pinnero, had been found shot to death in his midtown office. Although the case was still under investigation, police told reporters they believed the death was accidental, caused when Pinnero—apparently alone in his office at the time—was cleaning his .38 revolver, and shot himself in the chest. A photograph of Pinnero ran alongside the news account.

George Preston informed Inspector Hoskins of this latest development. The inspector's only comment was, "Well, I guess he can't verify Mrs. Carrolton's story, after all."

There, with several pieces of the puzzle missing, the question of who killed Evan McCallum rested unanswered.

Karen McCallum never did find out the solution to the hotel's Mystery Weekend before they all left London.

# CHAPTER SIX

AT THE TIME GEORGE Preston made hotel arrangements for the members of the board during their meeting in London, he had not, of course, anticipated how events would develop there. He had thought then that all of them might want a chance to relax afterward, and that it would be pleasant for them to return home by ship. So well in advance, he had booked passage for the twelve of them aboard the *Q.E. 2*.

There was one change in the plans: While George and Dina, Richard and Joanna, Kenneth and Karen, Anthony and Mitzi, Irene and Dr. Francke, and Liza Parkland would be occupying the cabins reserved for them, Evan would be returning in a coffin in the ship's hold. Nor could any of them have anticipated when they boarded the ship that by the time they disembarked in New York, they would have not one but two corpses on their hands.

It was a bit ironic that just after they experienced the hotel Mystery Weekend—which was supposed to have taken place aboard a fictitious ship—they should find themselves aboard a real ship.

As Karen McCallum remarked wryly on their first day at sea, "Let's hope we have smoother sailing than we did on the good ship S.S. *Van Dyne.*"

As was to be expected, they were all somewhat subdued from the first day out, staying pretty much together as a group. Most of them passed the time playing bridge or reading or sitting on deck.

From the first day out, it did not escape the notice of the others that Kenneth McCallum and Liza Parkland were virtually inseparable. The relationship apparently began when Kenneth tried to console Liza after the death of his brother, Evan. Very soon, however, it was clear that Kenneth and Liza were strongly attracted to one another.

It was at this time, too, that Liza dramatically turned from a blonde into a redhead. When several people in the group remarked on this striking transformation, Liza laughed and said, "Oh, it's just a wig— I have them in several colors and styles. Once in a while I wear one or the other to fit my mood, even though I'm a natural blonde. It's just a fun thing to do."

When Kenneth was not with Liza, he could usually be found with George. The two men used much of this unexpected free time to discuss and go over the materials they had collected for the book they hoped to write someday on the strange series of murders. And now, with Evan as yet another victim, they had one more case to add to their work. In addition to the meetings with Kenneth, George frequently stayed alone in his cabin revising and adding to the notes he was keeping on the murders.

On the afternoon of May 3, the sky was overcast and the sea choppy. Some of the group were in one of the ship's salons. Dina, Mitzi, Irene, and Liza were playing bridge. Valerie sat apart, knitting.

Afterward, when it would be important to know the whereabouts of each of them during that particular time period, it would be remembered that there had been a particular discussion during the bridge games. Dina had remarked that George was in their cabin; Mitzi had said that her husband, Anthony, had gone out on deck for a bit of air; Irene had mentioned that Dr. Francke was in his cabin reading a book; and Liza had told the others that she had stopped by the cabins of Karen and Kenneth before coming to the salon. Karen, according to Liza, said she was going to wash her hair, while Kenneth had told her he'd be along to the salon shortly.

Soon after this, Dina had looked up from her cards. Glancing toward the bar, she said, "Oh, there's Kenneth." Dina, wanting to drop out of the game, called over to the bar, "Hey, Kenneth! Come take my place."

The reply to her was a shake of the head, and Dina

thought: *Oh, well, he wants to have a drink in peace and quiet.*

Just about that time, Anthony Justin appeared. Dina made the same request of him, adding, "I want to go and haul George out of the cabin. He needs some diversion."

Dina left the salon and Anthony took her place at the bridge table.

It was not very long afterward that Dina came hurrying back to report that George hadn't answered her knocks and calls at his cabin door and that the door appeared to be locked from the inside. "I'm worried," Dina said. She said she had notified one of the ship's officers and that he had gone to get one of the maintenance crew to open the cabin door.

Dina left the salon quickly, followed by the seven of the group who were in the salon.

When they reached George and Dina's cabin, the maintenance man was already at work springing the lock to the cabin door. A ship's officer stood by, looking on.

After a couple of tries at the lock, the maintenance man nodded with satisfaction and swung the door open.

From the corridor outside the door, it was possible to see George sitting at the desk in the cabin, the upper part of his body slumped forward across the desk, the back of his skull crushed in. Lying on the desk top, not far from where his bloodied head rested, was a heavy cut crystal paperweight. One side of the paperweight had blood on it.

Dina cried out and ran forward. The others, be-

*A sketch of the Q.E. 2 cabin where George Preston was murdered*

hind her, reacted in various ways. Anthony, Valerie, and Irene crowded around the body next to Dina, and were joined by the ship's officer. Liza, who swayed on her feet and looked like she might faint, was helped back up the corridor away from the cabin by Mitzi. The maintenance crew man, his work done, scurried off in the opposite direction down the corridor.

As soon as the ship's officer had checked George's body and found no pulse, he immediately looked around the cabin, saying, "Is there any place here where someone could be hiding?"

Kenneth, who was standing in the doorway to the washroom, said, "I'd already thought of that." He motioned to the washroom, adding, "There's no one in there." He stepped aside to allow the ship's officer to see for himself that the washroom was empty. The ship's officer made a mental note that one of the cabin's portholes was slightly ajar. But he ruled out the possibility that anyone could have entered or left the cabin in that manner: The porthole was too high up for anyone to reach it without some means of aid, and there was nothing under the porthole now that could have been used for climbing upward.

"Could the cabin door have been locked from the outside by someone?" Kenneth asked.

The ship's officer shook his head. "No. That is not possible. The door was definitely locked from the inside."

Dina, still in a daze, made an irrelevant remark then: "I gave George the paperweight several years

*Paperweight used to kill George Preston. His wife had given him the paperweight, which he considered to be a lucky charm.*

ago. He always said it was kind of a lucky charm for him."

At that point the ship's officer herded them all out of the cabin and sent for the captain.

As soon as the captain made an inspection of the body and the cabin, he ordered the cabin locked up. He then hurried to the radio room and sent a message to the U.S. Coast Guard apprising them of the murder aboard.

Within a short time, a coast guard cutter pulled alongside the *Q.E. 2* and a party of four coast guard officers came aboard.

From that point on, the investigation into the murder of George Preston was intense.

All of those in the Hitchling Health Foods group were questioned and requestioned, but no one seemed able to provide a clue as to who killed George Preston or why. And since most of them had been together in the ship's salon at the time he was killed and could provide alibis for one another, there appeared to be no likely suspect. As for those who were absent from the salon, they satisfied the questioning officers as to their whereabouts: One of the crewmen had observed Anthony Justin out on deck at the time; one of the stewards had delivered a pot of tea to Dr. Francke in his cabin at the time; and when the officers went to Karen's cabin, she was drying her hair and seemed stunned by the news of George's death.

At the desk in the cabin where George had been sitting, officers found a thick notebook. This notebook, containing an almost complete record of the various past murders involving the group, also contained a full account of what George had been doing and whom he had seen earlier on that particular day.

*Calendar pad found on desk where George Preston was working when he was killed*

May 3—
Today I plan to get as much done as I can,
while still aboard ship, in revising the notes I am
compiling on the deaths of Judith Justin, William
Justin, Arthur Carrolton, Craig Sherwood, and Evan
McCallum. . . .

Later that same day, he wrote:

Kenneth and I just had a long session together
throwing theories back and forth about the five
deaths—or six, if we include the death of the private detective, Joe Pinnero. Kenneth thinks Pinnero *was* murdered, and the death made to look
accidental. He also believes that the shooting of
Pinnero is somehow connected to the other deaths
and/or murders. I'm not so sure. But I did give
Kenneth the memo from John Lange—concerning
Pinnero—that I received while I was on the Riviera before going to London. I hadn't had a chance
before to show the memo to Kenneth; he took it
away to make a copy so we'd each have one for
our files.

On the other hand, Kenneth doesn't believe
Craig Sherwood was murdered, and I'm inclined
to agree with him. Curiously enough, in that particular case we both think it wasn't connected to
the other deaths but was perhaps a coincidental
accident. Naturally, we both could be wrong, and
we agreed we'd have more discussion about it.
Kenneth remarked amusingly that if Sherwood was

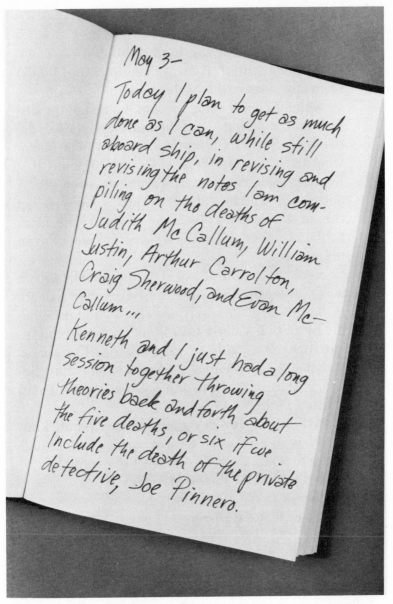

May 3—

Today I plan to get as much done as I can, while still aboard ship, in revising and revising the notes I am compiling on the deaths of Judith McCallum, William Justin, Arthur Carrolton, Craig Sherwood, and Evan McCallum...

Kenneth and I just had a long session together throwing theories back and forth about the five deaths, or six if we include the death of the private detective, Joe Pinnero.

*Notes George Preston was preparing at the time he was killed*

murdered, perhaps the butler—his butler, Timothy Grimes—did it. He wasn't serious, and I don't
seriously suspect the butler either.

Kenneth and I spent most of the rest of the discussion theorizing about the most recent case, the
death of Evan McCallum. I felt we were on somewhat tricky ground here since it is obvious that
Kenneth feels uncomfortable, perhaps even guilty,
about his brother's death. (This is because, of
course, Kenneth has become involved with Liza,
his late brother's fiancée; no secret to any of us in
the group.)

Kenneth is quite adamant in his belief that Evan
had nothing to do with Arthur Carrolton's death
in the plant in Pennsylvania. He is understandably bitter that Valerie Carrolton has spread the ru-
mor that Evan killed Arthur. Again, I'm not so
convinced that there wasn't any connection between Sherwood, Liza, and Evan (although I said
nothing of **this** to Kenneth).

We left off our discussion at this point. Kenneth has some film he took of various happenings
at the hotel in London, and has discovered he can
have the film developed on board.

Still later that day, George wrote:

I had lunch in the cabin and afterward was visited by Dr. Francke. He said he'd heard that Kenneth and I were collaborating on a possible book
about the murders and that he thought he'd like

to talk to me if I had time. I could not very well refuse him.

Like everyone else around, he had his own theories. He asked me if it had ever occurred to any of us that perhaps all the murders were being committed by someone totally outside the group?

I answered that, yes, I had had to consider that possibility but, in the absence of any clues pointing in that direction, I had gotten nowhere.

Just the same, he said, the possibility should be kept in mind.

Then he abruptly asked the most curious question: Had I ever thought that the murderer might be the least likely suspect in the group?

I answered that I had never thought in terms of most likely or least likely suspect.

His reply confounded me.

Perhaps I should think of the least likely suspect, he suggested. And he added—confounding me again—if I did, surely *he* would fit that category.

After all, he said, he was not joined to anyone else in the group by marriage or family, and he had no connection with Hitchling Health Foods. Did that not qualify him as least likely suspect, he wanted to know.

I felt he was toying with me then and, rather more coolly than I'd intended, I told him that I could easily figure out why he wasn't necessarily the least likely suspect. After all, he was connected to Irene (and for all I knew maybe one day they'd get married), and Irene was decidedly involved with the affairs of Hitchling Foods. That being the case, I added, he might just as well be a suspect, with motives, as any of the others of us.

He actually seemed to relish my answer. His parting words were that he'd like the two of us to get together again soon and further discuss him as a possible suspect.

After he left, I was annoyed with his visit. On the one hand, he could have been only tilting with me for the fun of it. But on the other hand, perhaps he had been deliberately egging me on to see if I had any real suspicions—and/or possible clues to back up those suspicions of him.

George ended his notes there, and for the moment the investigation into the murder of George Preston ended there as well—except for the continuing, dogged interest of John Lange. Once again, the problem for the private investigator was that he did not receive such evidence as existed until much later on.

# CHAPTER SEVEN

(AUTHORS' NOTE: *The file on the police investigation into the death of Anthony Justin—reprinted herewith—was obtained by Kenneth McCallum.*)

1. Tape recorded statement by Lieutenant L. R. Golenz, Connecticut State Police:

At 0500 hours this date, Troopers De Marco, Corliss, and I responded to a phone call from the horse farm owned by Anthony Justin, off Route II. Upon arrival, we found Anthony Justin dead as a result of gunshot wounds from a 12-gauge shotgun. (Facts later verified by the M.E.)

The victim lay on his back on a small sundeck just outside his first floor bedroom. He was wearing pajamas, robe, and slippers and had been shot in the chest. The shotgun (later verified as registered to him) lay on the sundeck approximately five feet away from his body.

Present in the house were the victim's wife, Margaret Justin, and several individuals identified as weekend guests: Richard and Joanna Durbin, Irene Durbin, Dr. Rupert Francke, Kenneth McCallum, Valerie Carrolton, and Liza Parkland.

After phoning in a report of what I had found, and requesting additional assistance, I took individual statements from all who were in the house at the time of the shooting.

### 2. Statement of Margaret (Mitzi) Justin:

Q.: *Please describe what happened.*

A.: I was asleep. I thought Justin was asleep beside me. We had gone to bed about 1 A.M. Suddenly, I was awakened by a loud noise. My heart was pounding. I guess I knew somehow it was the sound of a shot. I saw that Anthony wasn't in bed. I called out his name and then got out of bed. I saw that the door to the sundeck was open and I went out there. It was just about dawn, enough light so I could see. I saw him lying there. I went over to him to see if he was still alive. He wasn't.

Q.: *And that's when you got blood on your night-gown?*

A.: Where? I didn't notice—oh, I see. Yes, I guess that's when it must have happened.

Q.: *Did you touch him? Touch the body?*

A.: Touch—? No, I don't think so. I could see he was dead, was not breathing. I moved the gun—

Q.: *Wait! You moved the gun? Why?*

A.: It was lying across his body, across his chest. It looked—well, awful, obscene, you know?

Q.: *You moved the gun, where?*

A.: Where? To where it is now, leaning against the railing of the sundeck.

Q.: *Didn't you even consider the fact that you ought not to touch the gun?*

A.: No. I didn't think of it. I just thought he'd, you know, had an accident, had accidentally shot himself—

Q.: *Why would you think that?*

A.: The way he was lying, the gun was lying. I knew the shotgun was his. He kept it in the bedroom. We have some valuable horses in the stable out back.

Q.: *Go on.*

A.: When I saw him lying there, what I thought was he must have heard a noise, gotten up to investigate, and somehow, perhaps tripped and fallen, shot himself.

Q.: *And there was no one else around, you didn't see or hear anyone else around out there?*

A.: No.

Q.: *What happened then?*

A.: I screamed. And then everybody came running and

*Sundeck of Justin's Fairfield County farm. Chalk outline indicates where Anthony Justin's body was found.*

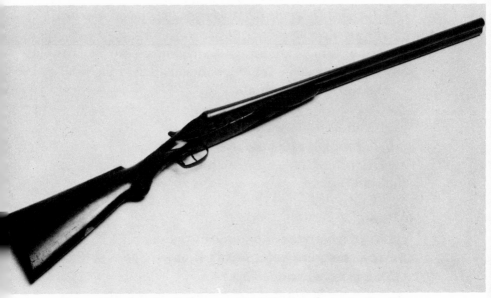

*Police photograph of shotgun that killed Anthony Justin. Gun was registered to Justin.*

then we called the police—called you.

Q.: *Can you think of anything else you'd like to add?*

A.: No. I can't think of anything else.

3. Statement of Valerie Carrolton:

Q.: *You told me you were the first one to reach the sundeck after the sound of the gunshot. Is that correct?*

A.: After the sound of two gunshots.

Q.: *Two shots? Are you sure?*

A.: I'm positive. I was awakened by the first shot. And while I was on my way out of the bedroom I heard the second shot.

117

Q.: *All right. Describe what you saw when you reached the sundeck.*

A.: I saw him, Anthony Justin, lying where he was when you came. There was blood all over the front, the top, of his bathrobe.

Q.: *Go on.*

A.: I could see he was dead.

Q.: *Go on. What else did you see?*

A.: His wife, Mitzi, was standing there.

Q.: *Standing how?*

A.: Standing by the railing on the sundeck, back from him.

Q.: *Near where the shotgun was leaning?*

A.: The shotgun? No, it wasn't leaning. She was holding it in her hands.

Q.: *She was holding the shotgun in her hands?*

A.: That's right, and then she leaned it up against the railing and she said something to me like: "There's been a terrible accident, Valerie. Anthony has accidentally shot himself."

Q.: *And then?*

A.: And then all the rest of them came running out of the house and then somebody, I think it was Richard, said we should call the police. And we did.

Q.: *When you first came out of the house, you didn't see or hear anyone else around?*

A.: Except for Mitzi, no.

Q.: *How long was it after you got to the sundeck before the others appeared?*

A.: How long? I'd say some minutes, several minutes, at least. Mitzi and I were there by ourselves.

*Single shotgun shell recovered by police after they arrived at Justin farm*

Q.: *How did you happen to arrive so quickly ahead of the others?*

A.: I can't say. Maybe because I was already up, out of bed, when I heard the first shot. I'm an early riser.

Q.: *You're sure about the two shots? You couldn't be mistaken?*

A.: I heard two shots.

Q.: *Can you think of anything else you'd like to add?*

A.: I don't know if I should say anything else—

Q.: *Anything else about what?*

A.: Well, about certain—certain things that happened—during the weekend between Mitzi and her husband, Anthony.

Q.: *Yes? What certain things?*

A.: Well, I mean should I talk to you about them now?

Q.: *If you think these things have any bearing on the shooting of Anthony Justin, please state them.*

A.: What it was, was that they'd been quarreling a lot.

Q.: *Go on.*

A.: I think it was about, well, about another woman, Liza Parkland—

Q.: *How do you know this?*

A.: The first afternoon we were here, we all went out horseback riding. During the ride I got separated from the others. After a while, I thought I was lost. I got down from my horse and led him, looking for a trail. We came to the edge of this clearing. Anthony, Anthony Justin, and Liza Parkland were in the middle of the clearing. They'd dismounted and were talking. I couldn't hear everything they said. He was holding her arm.

Q.: *Please go on.*

A.: I could see that he was very angry, and she was trying to pull away. He was saying something about she was making a big mistake. I heard him say the name "Kenneth"—that would be Kenneth McCallum, he and Liza have been together a lot in recent weeks. That seemed to be what Anthony was angry about. And then Liza pulled away from him and said something like "you don't own me." And then she got on her horse and left and so did he.

Q.: *Now tell me about the quarrels you said the Justins were having.*

A.: I haven't finished about that day, in the clearing. After Liza and Anthony rode away, I happened to glance across the clearing and I saw Mitzi Justin standing there, on the other side of the clearing. And I guessed she must have seen and heard everything I'd seen and heard. Then she, too, left. I don't think she even noticed me.

Q.: *Now, about the quarrels between the Justins?*

A.: That night, yesterday, and last night, I could hear their raised voices while they were in their bedroom. The room I'm in is right next to theirs. That's what I had to tell you.

Q.: *Is there anything else?*

A.: No. That's all. And I may have said too much as it is.


4. Statement of Liza Parkland:


Q.: *Describe what you heard and saw this morning from the time you awakened.*

A.: I was asleep when a noise awakened me. A sound like a loud bang. Later, I found out it was a shot.

Q.: *How many loud "bangs" did you hear?*

A.: One, I think. Then I could hear other people moving about, so I got up, put on my robe, and went to see what was going on.

Q.: *Continue.*

A.: When I got out to the sundeck, well, everybody

else was already there, and Anthony was—was there, like you saw him.

Q.: *You were the last person in the house to appear on the sundeck; why was that?*

A.: I guess, I suppose it was because the room where I was sleeping is on the other side of the house, the farthest away from the sundeck.

Q.: *Do you know of any trouble, any quarrels, recently between the Justins?*

A.: Mitzi and Justin? No. No. I don't.

Q.: *I've been told that you and Anthony Justin had angry words, a scene, on the afternoon of the first day you were here this weekend, while you were out horseback riding.*

A.: Anthony and me? No, I don't know what you're talking about.

Q.: *Someone claims to have observed you and Anthony together in a clearing, in the woods—*

A.: Who told you that? It's nonsense. I don't know what you're talking about!

Q.: *What was your relationship with Anthony Justin?*

A.: We were friends, Anthony and Mitzi and I, we were friends.

Q.: *And your relationship with Kenneth McCallum?*

A.: We're friends, too.

Q.: *Is there anything else you'd like to add?*

A.: No. Nothing.


5. Statement of Joanna Durbin:


Q.: *Please describe the events of this morning from the time you awakened.*

A.: I was brought awake by the sound of a loud noise—

Q.: *One loud noise, as you describe it, or two?*

A.: I really can't say, but I would think only one.

Q.: *And then what happened?*

A.: I awakened my husband, Richard—he's a sound sleeper—and we could hear other people moving around in the house. We went out to the sundeck; we could hear voices from there. Mitzi and Valerie were there—and of course poor Anthony.

Q.: *Did you know of any trouble between Margaret— Mitzi Justin—and her husband?*

A.: No. I did not.

Q.: *Didn't hear them having words at all this weekend?*

A.: No. I did not.

Q.: *Do you have anything else you'd like to add?*

A.: No. I do not.


### 6. Statement of Irene Durbin:

Q.: *Please describe the events of this morning from the time you awakened.*

A.: I was asleep in my room. There was a loud knock on the door. I got up. It was Dr. Francke. He said something seemed to have happened. We went together and found the others, Mitzi, Valerie, Richard, and Joanna, on the sundeck.

Q.: *You didn't hear any sound of a shot, or shots?*

A.: No, I didn't. Dr. Francke told me at the time he knocked on the door that he thought there had been a shot or shots fired from nearby.

Q.: *Do you have any knowledge of trouble between the Justins this weekend?*
A.: Trouble? I don't know anything about that.
Q.: *Do you know of anything else you'd like to tell me?*
A.: No.

### 7. Statement of Dr. Rupert Francke:

Q.: *Please describe the events of this morning from the time you awakened.*
A.: I heard the sound of a shot or shots—or it could have been an echo. I got up, went to Irene Durbin's room, got her up, and we went out to the sundeck. There were other people there, with the corpse.
Q.: *About the shots. Was it one or two?*
A.: I told you. It could have been an echo.
Q.: *Were you aware of any problems between the Justins this weekend?*
A.: No, I wasn't.
Q.: *Do you have any other information that might be helpful to this investigation?*
A.: Not that I can think of.

### 8. Statement of Richard Durbin:

Q.: *Describe what happened this morning from the time you awakened.*
A.: I think my wife already told you I was asleep. She woke me up. She said she thought something had happened.

Q.: *You didn't hear a shot, any shots?*

A.: No.

Q.: *Go on.*

A.: My wife and I went out to the sundeck where some of the others already were.

Q.: *Do you know of any troubles the Justins might have been having?*

A.: Lieutenant, I know why you're asking me that question. I've heard that my sister, Valerie Carrolton, has made certain allegations about certain things she claims have happened. May I say something here?

Q.: *Please. Go on.*

A.: Valerie hasn't been well, emotionally, lately. It's not serious, but frankly I think she—well, she imagines things. You understand?

Q.: *Go on.*

A.: I'm only trying to say that she could be mistaken about her facts sometimes—shall we say?

Q.: *Go on.*

A.: That's about it. I've said all I can think of to say.

Q.: *Nothing to add?*

A.: No.

### 9. Statement of Kenneth McCallum:

Q.: *Would you tell me what happened this morning from the time you awakened?*

A.: I was asleep. I heard a noise. I got up to investigate. I went to the sundeck. Mitzi, Valerie, Richard, Joanna, Irene, and Dr. Francke were there. That's all I know. Does that answer your ques-

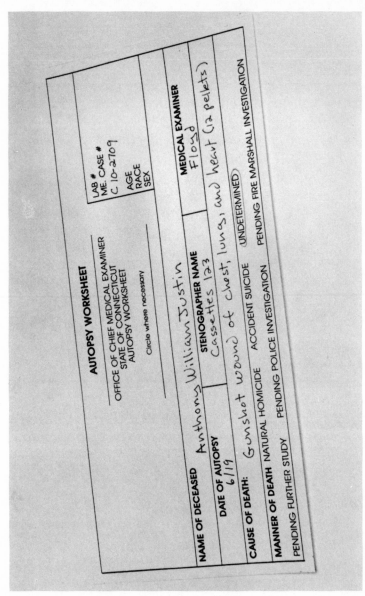

*Medical Examiner's worksheet prepared after autopsy on the body of Anthony Justin*

tions? Oh, I forgot to answer another question you've been asking everyone. No, I don't know of any trouble between the Justins. I know where you got that idea. Valerie should be careful of what she says. Other people can be harmed by her statements. Is there anything else, Lieutenant?

Q.: *No.*

# CHAPTER EIGHT

(AUTHORS' NOTE: *In order to complete a record of events for the next murder, John Lange requested a group interview with those persons still alive who had been involved in the story and who could supply information about the final death that occurred. Irene Durbin, Dr. Francke, Richard Durbin, Joanna Durbin, Karen McCallum, Dina Preston, and Liza Parkland all graciously consented to the interview. Valerie Carrolton declined. The interview took place in the Fifth Avenue offices of Hitchling Foods in Manhattan.*)

LANGE: First, I'd like to thank all of you for agreeing to talk with me. Ever since the death of George Preston, I've missed the notes and documentation

---

*Adler & Chastain*

he kept, which I hope will help me solve the murder. Now, with the assistance of so many of you who were present when the last death took place, I feel I'll have the complete story.

KAREN: Before we go on, I'd like you to know that Valerie Carrolton sends her apologies for not being here. She really hasn't been well. This interview might have been too much for her.

LANGE: I understand.

RICHARD: Where do you want us to start?

LANGE: I think it would be helpful to have some background leading up to the night of Kenneth McCallum's party.

RICHARD: Well, for some time now, ever since George Preston was—passed on, we, the board of Hitchling Health Foods, haven't had a chairman. As I understand it, Kenneth decided to have a get-together to try to select a new chairman and also to decide on new members of the board.

LANGE: That's right. You have been short-handed by several members, haven't you?

RICHARD: Yes. Anyhow, that, I guess, was the background to the party.

KAREN: Plus, I think, Kenneth also wanted to show off his new condominium apartment.

LANGE: Even though it wasn't finished yet?

KAREN: That was supposed to be the fun of it, something different.

IRENE: It was something different, all right! I was never so scared in my life, going up in that rickety contraption—

130

DR. FRANCKE: She means the construction elevators.

LANGE: For the record, why don't you tell me about that, about Kenneth's apartment—

DR. FRANCKE: Irene, you tell them.

IRENE: The building isn't even finished yet. It's still under construction; that is, all the floors are completed and the rooms laid out but they're still working on it.

DR. FRANCKE: That's why we had to use the construction elevators.

IRENE: Up forty-one floors, to the top, where Kenneth's apartment is situated. It was downright dangerous.

LANGE: You know, I wondered about that—

KAREN: Can I say something here?

LANGE: Yes, please. Anyone who has anything to say at any time, speak up.

KAREN: To Kenneth, the whole idea of having a party up there was that it would be fun! To have a party before the apartment, the building, was finished. Even with no furniture, and the floors bare concrete.

LIZA: It *was* fun, too! Kenneth had the party catered. A butler and three maids from the catering service brought folding tables and chairs along with the food and liquor. A few bare light bulbs provided the illumination—

DINA: And the view was spectacular!

KAREN: Come on, Irene, admit the view was worth the trip.

IRENE: Yes, the view was quite overwhelming.

LANGE: I saw one of the photographs taken from up there.

KAREN: I thought you might want to use it when I gave it to you.

*(AUTHORS' NOTE: It was Karen McCallum who supplied all the photographs used in this chapter.)*

JOANNA: What everybody's trying to say is that Kenneth had a novel idea in doing the party the way he did.

LIZA: Yes.

KAREN: And Kenneth enjoyed showing us through all the bare rooms of the apartment, showing us which rooms were which, and showing us the layout for the rooms from the building's plans.

LANGE: Just so I have it all straight: All of you were there?

LIZA: That's right. And Valerie, as well.

RICHARD: And after Kenneth had shown us the place, we had dinner, and discussed the company.

LIZA: Which was the whole purpose of the get-to-gether.

LANGE: And what did you decide?

RICHARD: We were all concerned that before we decided on a new chairman, we should fill the vacancies on the board. We all agreed, that is, those who were already members of the board—Kenneth, Valerie, Dina, and myself—that Irene, Karen, and Joanna should be elected to serve.

LANGE: As I understand it, the discussion was quite amicable.

*Spectacular photograph taken from Kenneth McCallum's new cooperative apartment in midtown Manhattan*

133

*The plans showing the layout of Kenneth McCallum's unfinished apartment*

RICHARD: I'd say so.

LIZA: Kenneth proposed a toast to the success of Hitchling Foods and everyone joined in.

KAREN: After dinner was served, the butler and maids removed the tables and chairs and left for the evening. Kenneth rode down in the elevator with them. He wanted to make sure they weren't delayed by the building's security guard in the lobby. Then Kenneth came back up.

LANGE: Did anything else happen after that?

RICHARD: It was close to midnight by then, so we all decided to leave.

LANGE: You left together?

LIZA: Explain about the elevators, somebody—Karen?

KAREN: There were two construction elevators that could be used, but neither of them was large enough to hold all of us. So we went down in separate groups.

LIZA: Irene, Dr. Francke, and I went down in one elevator.

KAREN: And Richard, Joanna, Valerie, and I went down together in another group. Dina stayed to ride down with Kenneth when one of the elevators returned.

LIZA: I would have stayed with Kenneth, only he suggested I go on ahead and get his car—which was parked in a garage a block away—and come back and pick him up.

DINA: After the others left, Kenneth and I had a short wait until one of the elevators returned. And then we went down.

LANGE: I understand that was the last anyone saw of Kenneth McCallum alive?

DINA: Yes. You see, what happened was that when Kenneth and I got to the lobby, they had one of those visitors' log books where you had to sign in and out. We both signed out and then, as we started toward the door, Kenneth suddenly stopped and said he'd forgotten his attaché case and he'd have to go back upstairs to get it. I offered to wait for him but he said for me to go on home. He said he'd have time to get up and back before Liza came to pick him up. I saw him get into the elevator and then I left.

LIZA: I must have gotten back to the building just after Dina left. There was no sign of Kenneth. The security guard wasn't at his desk either. I didn't know what to do. Finally, I rang for one of the elevators and went up to the apartment to look for Kenneth. As you know, he wasn't there.

LANGE: Meanwhile, wasn't something else going on?

RICHARD: You mean me? Yes, during all this I was stuck in the elevator somewhere up there between the lobby and the apartment. I was yelling my fool head off but nobody heard me.

BONNER: Explain how that happened.

RICHARD: We'd come down earlier, and just as Joanna and I started to get into a cab, I discovered I had the wrong attaché case; I had Kenneth's and I guessed he had mine.

JOANNA: As soon as Richard realized what had happened, he put me into a cab and sent me home, and he went back to Kenneth's apartment.

RICHARD: I signed in again in the lobby and went up

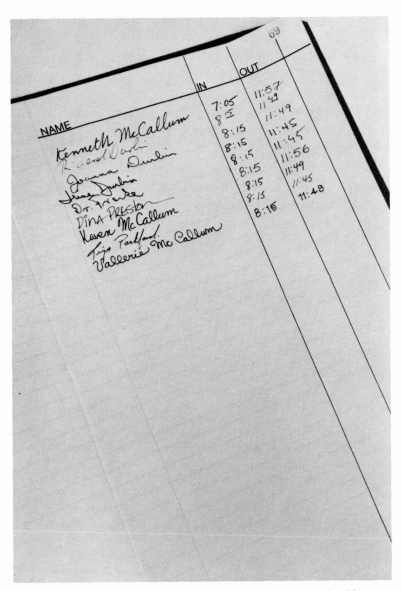

*Page from visitors' log book at Kenneth McCallum's building*

in the elevator and got stuck. It must have happened about the time Kenneth and Dina were coming down in the other elevator.

BONNER: But you never reached the apartment?

RICHARD: No. I got stuck on the way up.

LIZA: It wasn't until I was coming down, after I couldn't find Kenneth, that I heard Richard shouting from the other elevator as I went past. When I finally reached the lobby, I told the security guard and he went up and managed to rescue Richard.

RICHARD: And then we all began a search for Kenneth.

LIZA: I went out to a street phone and called Dina and everybody else to see if I could locate him. Nobody knew anything, but Valerie and Dina came back to the building to help look.

BONNER: And finally you called the police?

RICHARD: We did. And they came. And we spent most of the rest of the night looking.

KAREN: As you know, his body wasn't found until the next day.

RICHARD: Lying on top of one of the elevators. It was a freak accident. Apparently, after he went back up to the apartment and was on his way out, he accidentally stepped into an elevator shaft and fell forty-one floors to his death. That was the police verdict.

KAREN: A real tragedy.

RICHARD: And he had my attaché case with him.

IRENE: Well, Mr. Lange, that's the story. I know everyone here hopes it will be of help.

# Prominent Businessman Dies in Freak Elevator Accident

Kenneth McCallum, a member of the board of directors of Hitchling Foods, Inc., was found dead in the elevator shaft of the new building, still under completion, where he had recently purchased an apartment.

McCallum had given a small dinner party at his new apartment, said a representative of the building's management company, and apparently stepped into the elevator shaft by accident and plunged to his death.

Authorities are still investigating the curious circumstances of McCallum's fatal plunge.

Other members of the dinner party rode safely up and down the elevators, said a representative of the building's management company.

*Copy of newspaper clipping reporting the bizarre death of Kenneth McCallum*

LANGE: Yes, thank you for your cooperation. I appreciate your help. Now, I would appreciate it if all of you would remain here. I have a friend waiting outside. I'd like him to be present and to hear what I have to say next.

# CHAPTER NINE

JOHN LANGE WOULD state later that there was a definite stir of unease in the office when he brought his friend in and introduced him as "Captain Albert Rollins, Homicide, New York City Police Department."

Lange did not identify the three plainclothes detectives who accompanied the captain of homicide except to say, "And his associates."

Captain Rollins nodded pleasantly to the assembled group and took a place near the back wall of the room. The three other detectives stood near him, all four looking at Lange expectantly.

"Now see here!" Richard Durbin said in a gruff voice. "What exactly is this all about?"

"What this is all about," Lange answered in a level tone, "is the eight murders that have taken place among you, among us. I now believe I have solved all eight." He indicated the police officers. "And these gentlemen are interested in hearing what I have to say. As, I hope, all of you will be."

"I say that such a thing is impossible!" Dr. Francke exclaimed. "Too much time has passed since the first— ah—murder. If you've had proof of who committed all the crimes, dating back to the first one, why haven't you revealed your solutions before now?"

"The explanation of that is quite simple," Lange said. "The evidence, some of which is photographs, some written records, was only recently made available to me. And then too, I required time to make my deductions."

"So that now you believe you have actually solved all eight of these ghastly murders?" Dina Preston, who had asked the question, was clearly disbelieving.

"I think so, yes," Lange said.

Dr. Francke laughed. "This I have to hear."

"I, too," Captain Rollins added.

John Lange looked around at them, a small smile on his face. "And indeed you shall."

Lange walked to the center of the room, as would an actor in a play who wanted to command attention, which was his intention.

"You will have to follow me carefully now," Lange continued, "since we are going to reconstruct what happened in eight different situations, and it is my intention to do so in the sequence in which the eight murders occurred, starting with the first."

"I'm sure we can scarcely wait," Dr. Francke murmured.

Lange ignored Dr. Francke's words and instead said, "You will recall the first murder. On New Year's Eve at the Preston estate in Southampton, Long Island—"

"One could hardly forget," Dina Preston whispered.

Lange nodded. "The victim, Judith McCallum Justin, was found suffocated in a linen closet on the second floor of the Preston house. There was a plastic bag wrapped tightly around her head and face. The most mystifying element of the events that night was that you, Mrs. Preston, discovered the body first in the bedroom, and only moments later, I rushed into the bedroom to find the body had vanished!"

Dina Preston nodded.

"None of us could figure out how the body could have been removed so swiftly from the bedroom to the linen closet," Lange said.

"Not even the police," Captain Rollins interrupted. "I saw their reports."

"Not even the police," Lange said. "The explanation is that *the body was never in the bedroom!* You, Mrs. Preston, only *claimed* to have seen it."

Dina shook her head. "Why should I do that?"

Lange walked toward her. "For the best reason in the world. To protect the murderer." He paused for a moment before saying, "Judith McCallum Justin's murderer was your husband: George Preston. He killed her with the plastic bag and hid her body in the linen closet; then you screamed to the household that her body was lying in the bedroom. A ploy to distract the eye."

"Why would George Preston have killed Judith?" Richard Durbin asked.

"Simple." Lange answered. "She wanted to take over his company, Hitchling Health Foods. And would have succeeded no doubt, had she lived. Those facts were known."

"You have no proof," Dina Preston said. "No evidence."

"Yes, I do." Lange's voice was firm. "There was a print discovered on the closet shelf—"

"Which was never identified by the police," Captain Rollins pointed out. "And they had George Preston's fingerprints."

"It was *not* a fingerprint," Lange said sharply. "It was the print left by a rubber finger guard worn by George Preston—"

"How can you know this?" Dina was quite agitated now.

"Because"—and here John Lange removed from a large envelope two photographs—"that print exactly matches a print found on a memo sent by me to George Preston, which he read and upon which he made notes. He was wearing the rubber finger guard while he made notes on the memo." Lange held up the two photographs. "You can clearly see that the two prints match." (EDITOR'S NOTE: The two photographs can be found in this book, the first in Chapter 1 and the second in Chapter 4.)

Dina whirled toward the door to the office but two of the N.Y.P.D. plainclothesmen had already moved to bar the door.

"Your husband killed Judith McCallum Justin," Lange said to Dina. "And you were an accessory to the murder."

Dina collapsed into a nearby chair.

"So," said Lange, "we have now disposed of the first murder."

"I must say," Richard Durbin spoke up, "you have astounded us all with your deductions."

John Lange gave a gracious tip of his head in acknowledgment. "Next," he went on, "we come to the second murder. At the ski lodge in Aspen, Colorado, owned by Craig Sherwood, who was also chairman of Triplex, Incorporated. This time the victim was William Justin."

Lange moved away from Dina Preston and slowly paced the office as he said, "The most complete record we have of what went on at the ski lodge in Aspen came from a report written by George Preston, a report he hoped to have published, according to a note he included in the report."

"We've all read it," Kenneth McCallum remarked.

"And very thorough it was," Lange said. "To refresh your memories, you will recall it was George Preston who discovered William Justin's body in Justin's bedroom, the spike end of a ski pole embedded in the chest."

"But with no indication of who killed him," Dr. Francke said.

Lange held up a hand. "Not quite so. Actually, if

one reads Preston's report with a sharp enough eye, one will find the identity of the murderer there."

"I confess I didn't find it," Captain Rollins said.

Lange took a sheet of paper from his coat pocket. "Let me read you a few sentences written by George Preston. Quote: 'I slid [the door] open and went inside. . . . It still appeared that the room was empty. . . . I spotted Justin lying, asleep I guessed, on a chaise lounge. . . . Before I could move I thought I heard a sound outside. . . .' Unquote." Lange glanced up from the paper. "Preston then wrote of how he waited, listening for the sound outside, and then wrote: Quote: 'Later, when I would try to recall how long I was in the room, I couldn't possibly calculate. . . . What I saw clearly then, for the first time, was that Justin lay on the chaise lounge—quite dead—the spike of a ski pole embedded deeply in his chest. . . .'"

Lange stopped reading and returned the sheet of paper to his coat pocket.

"I read all of that," Dr. Francke said impatiently. "I saw no mention of Justin's murderer there."

"It's there," Lange said. "In the murderer's own words. Preston wrote that he, Preston, entered the room and saw Justin asleep on the chaise, that he heard a sound outside, that some time passed, and that he then turned on the light and saw Justin's body, the spike of the ski pole embedded in Justin's chest. In the time that passed between Preston's entering the room and turning on the light, he, Preston himself, killed Justin."

"And George Preston wrote his account to divert

146

suspicion away from himself," Captain Rollins pointed out.

"Exactly," Lange agreed. "It's a device that has been used in mystery fiction."

"And the motive?" Rollins asked.

"Again," Lange said, "it was the danger of losing the Hitchling Health Foods Company. Justin, you will remember, was out to merge it with Triplex, Incorporated, Craig Sherwood's company, and Preston would have lost control."

"What about the ordeal Karen McCallum experienced in Aspen, her kidnapping?" Richard Durbin asked.

"She *was* kidnapped," Lange answered. "Exactly as she said. George Preston and Dina here kidnapped her briefly in hopes that no one would believe her story, and therefore everyone would suspect she had been at the ski lodge all along. Since they look so much alike, it would be suspected that she had changed places with her twin, enabling *him* to kill Justin. In other words, Preston hoped that's what would be suspected. But that did not happen. George Preston killed Justin."

"All right," Richard Durbin said. "I, for one, am satisfied that you have the correct solutions to the first two murders. What about the others?"

John Lange took a deep breath before he spoke. "The solutions to the remaining six murders are interconnected. The murders of Arthur Carrolton, of Craig Sherwood, of Evan McCallum, of George Preston, of Anthony Justin, and—finally, the eighth mur-

147

der—of Kenneth McCallum. To solve each in turn requires reference to the others, since it will be necessary to my solutions to skip back and forth among them and for you to carefully follow my reasoning." (EDITOR'S NOTE: The reader of this book can follow John Lange's reasoning by referring to the various events in the book as he explains.)

"To the third victim, then," Lange said. "Arthur Carrolton, who met his death in the Hitchling Health Foods laboratories. Anthony Justin was the killer."

There were several exclamations from around the room. Lange waited for them to subside before he continued.

"Valerie Carrolton honestly believed Evan McCallum was the killer. If you will recall the later death of Evan in London at the hotel during the so-called Mystery Weekend, you will find that she named him as Arthur Carrolton's killer." (EDITOR'S NOTE: These facts are included in Chapter 5 of this book.)

John Lange paused, and then said, "Actually Anthony Justin killed Arthur Carrolton for the reasons Valerie stated, only she had the wrong murderer. It was Justin who was photographing the formula. Carrolton walked in on him and Justin killed him."

"And you've determined how Carrolton was killed?" the police captain, Rollins, asked.

"Yes," Lange said. "In one of the photos, taken by the Minox camera, you will see the murder weapon." Lange produced the photo and pointed. "The coat hanger. Justin snatched it up, twisted it around Carrolton's neck, then returned it to its place in the office."

"I would like to point out," Liza Parkland said, "that Valerie also claimed I was working with Evan McCallum; she was wrong about that."

"She was," Lange agreed. "Actually you, Liza Parkland, were working with Anthony Justin."

"I had nothing to do with the death of Arthur Carrolton," Lisa said.

"That may be true," Lange agreed again. He then spoke rapidly: "However, in the case of the next victim—the fourth, Craig Sherwood—you were an accessory. Craig Sherwood was killed by Anthony Justin." (EDITOR'S NOTE: Facts corresponding to Lange's conclusions are to be found in Chapter 4 of this book.)

John Lange stared intently at Liza Parkland as he continued: "Justin and you went to Sherwood's town house. Justin knocked out Sherwood and you and Justin then carried the inert body to the bathroom and drowned him in his shower."

"The evidence—?" Liza asked.

"Ah, yes," Lange nodded. "First, the motive. Valerie was telling everyone she knew who killed *her* husband, Arthur Carrolton. Justin was afraid she knew he was that killer and could prove it if he was connected up with Sherwood, so he had to eliminate Sherwood."

"The evidence—?" Liza asked again.

"Justin admitted he was at Sherwood's house that evening. No one else could be placed there—except you, Ms. Parkland. That strange print in the spilled powder, and a fingerprint found in the house—"

"What about them?" Liza asked.

"Both were yours." Lange took three photographs from an envelope. "The print in the powder was your heel print. And though that might be difficult to prove, the fingerprint isn't. See here." He showed a photograph. "This is a shot of the fingerprint found in Sherwood's house. And here"—he held up another photograph—"a shot of a fingerprint next to your name where you signed out in the visitors' log at Kenneth McCallum's apartment building." (EDITOR'S NOTE: Photographs of the prints can be found in Chapters 4 and 8 of this book.) "Also," Lange added, "you were the woman in the black wig seen by Craig Sherwood's neighbors."

At these words, Liza Parkland collapsed into a chair.

"Anthony Justin," John Lange said, "was also the murderer of Evan McCallum in London. Justin pushed Evan from the hotel window. The reason was that when Valerie pushed the note under the door to Evan's room, Evan knew immediately that Liza Parkland had not been working with *him*, and he guessed she had been working with Justin. Justin had to kill Evan to keep Evan from connecting him—and Liza—to Sherwood's murder. Simple, when you add up all the evidence."

"Simple for you, maybe," Richard Durbin said. "Are you going to tell us now that the next victim, George Preston, was also killed by Justin?"

John Lange shook his head. "No. Preston was killed in his cabin aboard the *Q.E. Two* out of a motive for revenge."

The Picture-Perfect Murders

"Revenge?" Karen McCallum asked.

"Revenge," Lange repeated, "for the earlier murder of Judith McCallum Justin, your mother."

Lange glanced around the room before fixing his eyes on Karen as he declared, "George Preston had his skull smashed in by a paperweight wielded by your twin brother, Kenneth McCallum."

Lange again withdrew from his pocket some papers. "As we can see from notes left by George Preston, he gave a copy of my memo to Kenneth to read. As soon as Kenneth saw the print of the rubber finger guard, worn by Preston, on the edge of the memo, he recognized it as the print that had been found on the plastic sheet that had been used to suffocate his mother—and he knew George Preston had killed her."

"But the door to Preston's stateroom was locked from the inside," Rollins pointed out.

"True," Lange said. "But I would remind you of the whereabouts of everyone just prior to the discovery of Preston's body inside the locked stateroom." (EDITOR'S NOTE: Lange here is referring to the accounts of events in Chapter 6.)

Lange looked at Karen McCallum. "It was *thought* at the time that Kenneth was in the lounge. He wasn't, however. It was Karen here who was in the lounge, disguised as her twin, Kenneth. After the locked cabin was entered, Karen—disguised as Kenneth—disappeared from the corridor without being noticed. Once everyone was in the cabin, Kenneth very cleverly appeared. Everyone, attention directed toward Preston's body, assumed—when Kenneth spoke to say no

151

one was hiding in the bathroom—that he too had come in from the corridor. *In actual fact, he had smashed in Preston's skull, locked the stateroom door from the inside, and hidden in the bathroom, emerging as if he had searched there for a possible killer."*

Lange lowered his head, then looked up at Karen. "I'm sorry you had to be an accessory."

"And what of the death of Anthony Justin, Mr. Lange?" Dr. Francke asked.

"His murder was a relatively straightforward case," Lange said, "if one read the evidence clearly."

"Revenge again?" Captain Rollins inquired.

"No," Lange said. "But the motive was almost as old as that of revenge; it was jealousy."

"One of the most ancient of motives," Dr. Francke added.

"Margaret 'Mitzi' Justin killed her husband, Anthony Justin," Lange said. "She was jealous of his relationship with you." Lange pointed to Liza Parkland. "You see, the story told by Valerie McCallum about you, Liza, and Justin was true and about the quarrels Justin and his wife had the evening before. True in every respect." (EDITOR'S NOTE: Here and elsewhere in Lange's explanation, the details are to be found in Chapter 7 of this book.)

Lange removed some photographs and pages from his envelope. "At the time, the evidence was recorded in two places. There were two shots, meaning it was deliberate, and that's why when Valerie first got to the sundeck, Mitzi Justin was still holding the shotgun in her hands. The proof that two shots had been fired—although Mrs. Justin denied this—is contained here, in the autopsy report on Anthony Justin. It says, Quote: 'Cause of death: gunshot wound of chest, lung, and head,' and in parentheses *twelve pellets*. You understand?"

Several people in the office shook their heads.

"The clue," Lange said, "is that a single shotgun round contains *only nine pellets, so two shots had to have been fired.* Mrs. Justin produced only one shell, having hidden the other one so it would look as if her husband had shot himself accidentally. But he didn't. She shot him twice, and it was no accident. The police have already picked her up, at my suggestion."

"And now we come to the most recent, the eighth and final murder." Lange's voice now sounded tired.

"Kenneth McCallum's death," Richard Durbin said.

"Correct." Lange nodded. "And, once again, the motive is revenge. Revenge for revenge, just as Kenneth McCallum killed George Preston because Preston killed Kenneth's mother, Judith. You see, Kenneth wasn't the only one who made a connection between Preston's prints on the plastic bag and on the sheet of the memo. When you"—here Lange turned to Dina Preston—"found your husband, George Preston, dead, you realized that Kenneth McCallum had killed him because McCallum had discovered your husband had killed his mother."

"I did not kill Kenneth," Dina Preston said in denial.

"You caused his death," Lange said coldly. "It comes to the same thing."

"You can't prove—" Dina started to say.

"I can prove it," Lange said flatly. "You were the last one upstairs with Kenneth. You took the construction elevator down alone, so that when he went to enter the elevator in the dark it was already gone and he fell into the elevator shaft and down it to his death."

"But he signed out," Richard Durbin interjected.

"He *did not* sign out," Lange said sharply. "Further proof that you, Mrs. Preston, caused his death. The truth is *you* signed *him* out because he was already dead. Ask me how I can prove it."

When Dina remained silent, Lange continued: "Here I have the visitors' log signed that night by all of you. You will note that the time signed out next to Kenneth McCallum's name is eleven fifty-seven. You will further note how the figure seven is written." (EDITOR'S NOTE: Lange is speaking of the photograph of the visitors' log in Chapter 8.)

Lange held up another page as he said, "And here I have a calendar removed from George Preston's stateroom aboard the *Q.E. Two*. On it he wrote: 'Dinner when? Dina?' and underneath this is the figure *seven*, written in by you in the same fashion as you wrote it in the visitors' log next to Kenneth Mc-Callum's name." (EDITOR'S NOTE: Here Lange is referring to a photograph of the calendar pad included in Chapter 6 of this book.)

John Lange had reached the end of his recital.

Captain Rollins stepped forward. "Now," he said, "it is my turn." He looked around the room at those

# NEW HEAD OF HITCHLING FOODS

It was announced today that Richard Durbin has been elected President and Chairman of the Board of Hitchling Foods, Inc.

Hitchling Foods, Inc. is among the leading health food companies internationally.

Richard Durbin takes over the company at a time when there are rumors that it was the target of a hostile take-over.

Durbin, through a prepared press release, said: "I look forward to serving Hitchling Foods, Inc. as President and Chairman and shall strive to uphold the tradition and quality of service long established by this organization.

The election of Richard Durbin to the post was greeted by Wall Street analysts as a stabilizing influence on the company's future.

*Copy of newspaper clipping announcing the election of Richard Durbin as chairman of the board of Hitchling Health Foods*

155

Adler & Chastain

who had been implicated in the eight murders and added, "All of you will have to go with me for further questioning." He made a motion with his hand to his men to round up those who had been accused. Then he said to Lange, "I congratulate you. Is there anything else?"

"Nothing," Lange said. "The rest is up to you and the courts. . . ."

# EPILOGUE

IN THE TIME SINCE THE death of Kenneth McCallum, the Hitchling Health Foods Company has prospered, its stock selling at an all-time high. Richard Durbin is currently chairman of the board.